# Praise for BO'S CAFÉ

"BO'S CAFÉ is more than the riveting story of a talented young businessman and a striking woman trying to keep their marriage and his thriving career together. What one reads actually shifts the foundation of the way we view the world, the way we reconcile our relationships, and how we define success. Groundbreaking. Soul-filling. Life changing. This is a story that will not let go of you."

**—Wes Roberts, CCO, Leadership Design Group**

"Everyone needs to pull up to the counter at BO's CAFÉ. It's the safest place on earth to work through some of the most dangerous issues of your life."

**—Tim Kimmel, author, *Grace-Based Parenting***

"In a world obsessed with projecting the 'perfect' image, it's not surprising that women are facing a crisis of identity these days. What is startling, however, is that we are not alone. BO'S CAFÉ offers a window into the private hell of a man's fear of inadequacy and makes a compelling case for the power of grace through relationship to set things right for us all."

**—Constance Rhodes, author, *Life Inside the "Thin" Cage* and *The Art of Being***

"Real, witty, profound. This book should be required reading for all mentors! BO'S CAFÉ moves you to trust the love you have been freely given, to pursue the freedom it provides, and to start experiencing a life that most men and women miss—the way of authenticity, integrity, and joy."

**—Carson Pue, author, *Mentoring Leaders***

"I cried when Lindsey first hugged Andy, and when Steven confessed to Lindsey, and when Steven realized that Andy was his trusted friend, and when I wondered whom I was controlling through my anger. Kleenex, please."

—**Bill Hull, coauthor,** ***Choose the Life***

"Until we realize that we fall short of perfection and accept the unconditional love of God and the imperfect love of others available to us, we will continue to struggle through life. BO'S CAFÉ is a wonderful story that will help you in your journey to true fulfillment."

—**Ken Blanchard, coauthor,** ***The One Minute Manager®*** **and** ***Lead Like Jesus***

"BO'S CAFÉ challenges my own authenticity in leadership and encourages me to continue to find room and grant space for greater grace in my own daily living and interaction with others caught in the realities, disappointments, surprises, and challenges of life and faith."

—**Commissioner Lawrence R. Moretz, territorial commander, USA East, Salvation Army**

"BO'S CAFÉ is not a *free ride.* It is a ride to freedom. In BO'S CAFÉ you will find a grace more powerful than willpower or tenacity. You'll find a safe place in God that can handle our deepest wounds and most persistent sins."

—**Todd Hunter, coauthor,** ***Christianity Beyond Belief***

"What if you could reveal your worst fears and flaws and discover there are those who still believe in you? This is the power of BO'S CAFÉ—an authentic community where the unlikely are transformed. Pick up this terrific book and take a seat at the table of grace."

—**Drs. Les and Leslie Parrott, founders of RealRelationships.com and authors of** ***Love Talk***

# BO'S CAFÉ

JOHN LYNCH,
BILL THRALL, *and*
BRUCE McNICOL

www.boscafe.com

This book is a work of fiction. Names, characters, places, and incidents are the product of the author's imagination or are used fictitiously. Any resemblances to actual events, locales, or persons, living or dead, is coincidental.



Published by Windblown Media
4680 Calle Norte
Newbury Park, CA 91320
E-mail: office@windblownmedia.com
Phone: (805) 498-2484 Fax: (805) 499-4260

Published in association with Hachette Book Group, Inc.

Printed in the United States of America

First Edition: September 2009
10 9 8 7 6 5 4 3 2

Library of Congress Control Number: 2009924635

ISBN 978-1-935170-04-4

*Dedicated to all the "Andys" who have been creating Bo's Cafés for "Stevens" everywhere.*

# BO'S CAFÉ

# Fenton's —ill

*(Wednesday Evening, March 11)*

"They just never let up, do they?"

He's sitting right next to me—a guy about my dad's age—with a tall glass of ice in front of him. He's watching the tiny television bolted to the wall in the corner of the bar, balancing his chair with a flip-flopped foot propped up against the counter.

A dozen empty chairs, and this guy's sitting next to me. I get up and move a couple of stools over. I glance at him just long enough to size him up. He's scruffy-looking, wearing an old Dodgers ball cap, ragged Levi's, and a loud Hawaiian shirt. He looks like he's been following Jimmy Buffett on tour. Old guys like this are all over Southern California. It's as if they're scattered around strategically by the Department of Tourism.

"Sometimes it's hard to figure, isn't it?" he says, his eyes fixed on the TV.

*Is this guy talking to me? I think he's talking to me.* "I'm not really watching the game."

Still staring, he says through a mouthful of ice, "I'm not talking about the game."

*I just need to stay quiet. He'll figure out I want to be left alone.*

"You're not a regular here."

I glance over at him. "No."

"No," he repeats.

"Look, no offense, but I'd really like to be alone."

He waves his hand. "No, hey—don't let me bother you there, champ. You just keep at what you're doing. Pretend I'm not here."

There's a pause, and then he starts in again. "Yep, I've got my ice. Tall glass of ice, that's what I've got. Nothing better than nature's own H-2-O. Am I right?"

*Can't this guy take a hint?* I stare down at the bar, willing him to be quiet.

"Cold, clean, no aftertaste. Just God's own beverage. *Agua.* Yep, that's my drink—*el agua*. It means 'the water' in Spanish. Those folks make a big deal out of the definite article, don't they?" He shakes his glass and looks through it. "A lot of people might think *el agua* just means 'water.' Those same people would be wrong. It's *the* water, isn't it?"

He looks over at me again. "Oops. Sorry. I'm bothering you, aren't I? Look, you just pretend I'm not here."

Not even twenty seconds pass.

"Truth be told, it's not the water, really. It's the ice. They say it's bad for your teeth, but I love it. Crunching it. You know, the ice."

I shouldn't be here. I should be home, watching the news with my wife and daughter after dinner. Instead, I'm sitting here, listening to some lonely old hippie chew ice.

"Here" is a restaurant in east Culver City that has changed hands more often than a cafeteria tray. Its present name is Fenton's Grill. On the sign out front, the neon *Gr* is blinking in and out, so the display sporadically reads *Fenton's ill.* From the looks of the place, it's easy to see why he would be.

When I was a kid, Fenton's wasn't even Fenton's. It was Petrazello's—a friendly neighborhood restaurant, clean, homey, and reasonably priced. Even after dark I felt safe walking there. It was always the centerpiece of life in the ten or so square blocks of my childhood world. Little League teams would wolf down pizza there. Dates sat stiffly in rented outfits at white-linen-covered tables. I was one of them, sitting across from gorgeous Brenda Magnusson. A perspiring freshman in an ill-fitting suit about to go to homecoming, where the entire world would discover that I couldn't dance. Other nights the place transformed into a loud, smoky den where husbands gathered around a television set in the bar, praising or berating the Dodgers. The women sat nearby, praising and berating their husbands.

Old man Petrazello was always there, day or night, greeting the neighborhood at the cash register or on busy nights reworking tables to jam as many into that room as the fire marshal would allow. Nobody ever seemed to mind how crowded it was. Nobody seemed in a hurry at Petrazello's. You were in a room with familiar faces. Friends of your parents walking by your table, tousling your hair, calling you by a nickname, and telling you they saw the double you hit last game.

Old man Petrazello carried candy in a pocket of his apron for the kids. Good candy. Not the cheap mints they put up front for a donation to the Civitans. Old man Petrazello was always smiling too. It's as if he didn't run the place for a profit but because he truly enjoyed being a relative to everyone in our neighborhood.

But that was then, and this is now.

The once attractive freestanding building with a few parking spaces and some nice landscaping was eventually asphalted over, and some other cheap buildings were added to form a strip mall. Fenton's is now more bar than restaurant. The TV is still in the same spot—maybe even the same one, judging by the bent antenna. The lighting is a strange combination of harshly glaring and dim. I have no idea how that effect is achieved, but it can't mask the fact that the floor is the same drab green linoleum I remember. Every few feet along the bar—now Formica instead of wood—are mismatched plastic dishes of Spanish peanuts. One bowl has little tiki faces. Another says, "Visit Arizona!"

The "grill" is several wobbly tables with plastic vases of plastic flowers. So I opted for the bar.

Fenton's is about eight miles from where I work—not far by Southern California standards, but I hadn't come down here in years until recently. I guess it's embarrassing to see what my childhood world has become. My old neighborhood is on the decline—one in a long list of once proud middle-class communities falling victim to quick-cash stores and porn shops. Taking the surface streets from my office in Santa Monica, the scenery quickly morphs from manicured curbsides and executive condos to a conveyor belt of sputtering neon.

But now, for the first time in a long time, I'm actually inside this joint. The first two times I ended up in the parking lot and didn't even get out of the car. I just sat there, angry, resentful, and noisy. Arguments at home, conflicts at work all rattling around in my head. And this horrible feeling that I can't drive far enough to get away from it. Something is wrong. Something's not working, when everything *should* be working. I don't know how to describe what I'm feeling. It's like coming to a place in your life where all the slot lines come up cherry but nothing comes out of the machine. You sit there, hoping that staring will make something happen.

*I'm here again,* I thought, *and I'm hungry. Fenton's "illness" aside, I might as well see what this place has sunk to.*

Everything on the menu looks a little scary. This is not a place where you gamble on meat loaf.

The bartender is impatient even though he has few other customers.

"I'll have a manhattan."

Why did I say that? I'm not even sure what a manhattan is. I think my dad used to drink them. Something about Fenton's wood-paneled decor suggests that a *manhattan* might be an appropriate drink for a person who doesn't want to stand out.

A half dozen or so patrons are engaged in muffled conversations. The place looks smoky, though I know the smoking ban in California makes that impossible. It's as if all the smoke of years past is still hovering in the air. Or maybe it's grease from the grill. The surface of the bar feels a little filmy.

My manhattan appears, and I'm quickly acquainted with why I've never ordered one. It tastes like butane with a splash of syrup. I ask for a glass of water and mindlessly stare at the sports recap on the television.

That's when the scruffy-looking guy sat down... I think.

*Okay, what can I say without sounding like a jerk so he'll get the message? Why do guys like this go into bars and try to start conversations with complete strangers?*

"She got to you last night, didn't she?"

"What?" My head whips in his direction.

"Last night."

Now I'm getting ticked. "*Who* got to me? What are you talking about?"

"Your wife," he says. "You knew she was right, of course. Same stuff. But no way were you gonna own it. What would you do, anyway? Say you're sorry and repeat the same thing next week? I can see why you drink."

"I'm *not* drinking!" I nearly shout. "I mean, I'm not a drinker." I put some cash on the bar and get up.

"Sure... lots of guys come in a bar and order stiff drinks by name because they're not drinkers. Listen, sport, you're not obligated to explain anything to me. Most people don't want to deal with what's eating at them. Just pretend I'm not here."

*This guy has just called me "champ" and "sport." What's next, "chief"?*

"Your wife," he says flatly. "The argument. The whole reason you drove down here instead of going home after work. I mean, this is a long way from Manhattan Beach."

I turn and look at him. "What was that?"

"Gotcha there, didn't I?" he says with a grin. "Pretty hard to just get up and leave when a total stranger starts reeling off details about your life. Am I right?"

He walks over to me and puts his hand on my shoulder, like he's about to tell an old friend a joke. In one move I push his hand off me and step back.

"Get away from me. You don't know me!"

For a moment the room is frozen, my words hanging in the air.

He raises his hands, palms toward me. "Whoa, whoa, whoa there, partner. Calm down. I'm just talking."

Just as I get to the door he calls to me. "You gonna just up and leave? You come to this place for maybe the third time in as many months and finally stumble inside. You're telling me some guy starts throwing out some pretty accurate details about your life, someone who takes an interest in you and the problems that got you here... *and you walk?*"

"What?" I turn back from the door. "What are you saying to me?"

"Look, you're making me strain my voice here, chief," he says. "You want to talk, then come sit back down with your nonalcoholic manhattan."

I walk back to the counter. *What am I doing talking to this nut? I don't want to talk to anyone.* I sit down in front of the flammable drink.

"—even if he could tell you why you're so sad?"

"Listen. Who are you, Mister?"

"I just thought you might be thinking something along those lines. See if this fits: It's like you're stumbling around in a dark room, bumping into furniture. How am I doing? Making sense?"

I stare at him blankly.

"I'll take your silence as a yes."

His voice gets quieter and lower. "After many experiences, you've learned to memorize paths around the pain. You think you've finally figured out how to navigate in the dark. You almost get used to doing life in the dark. Then the next day, week, month, maybe while you're sleeping, the furniture gets moved, and you slam your shin into an end table.

"And each time, with each new bruise, you lose more and more hope, more confidence, more sense of purpose. You start reacting to pain more than anything else. You make decisions based on what hurts least. You avoid stuff you know you should face. You avoid interaction with people you suspect might be moving your furniture. Eventually that list grows to include a whole lotta people.

"And the worst part is that it feels like almost everyone else can see you stumbling around. It's like they can all see the furniture. They might never tell you this, but you're pretty sure they know."

He looks at me, waiting, but I've lost my response. He turns back to the television. "So how am I doing, Steven?"

"How do you know my name?"

He ignores my question. "They want to tell you, you know."

"Who does?"

He taps the bar with his fingertips. "Your friends. Your family. Those you work with. Truth is, some of them have actually tried. They want to help. But you don't believe they can help. Sound familiar, Steven?"

I sit up straight on my stool and nearly knock over my glass of water. "Look, I don't know who you think I am, but I don't know you. Now stop the game, pal, and tell me how you know *me*."

No response.

I pick up my water glass and lean closer to him. "You want me to call the manager? Or do you want me to pour this glass of ice all over you before I throw you out in the street?"

His voice is quieter now. "Yeah, I guess you could do that. Then you could drive home and pretend this didn't happen. You could go back to what you've been doing. Pretend it's just a bad week, a couple bad breaks. But you'll be back. If not here then somewhere else."

He pauses.

"And until you let someone shine a light into your room, nothing's gonna change. Life's gonna get more painful, more confusing, and darker. Pour ice on me if you want. Heck, throw me out if it makes you feel better."

The man tips up his glass and shakes a couple of ice cubes into his mouth.

"Oh, by the way, you might wanna take that name tag off your shirt if you don't want strangers calling you by name, Steven. . . . Just a thought."

I look down and see the name tag—the little sticker with my name on it that I've worn all day since that meeting outside the office. *What an idiot!* Might as well have been wearing a sign around my neck saying, "Please talk to me, I'm lonely!" I rip the sticker off my shirt.

We're both quiet, except for his obnoxious crunching.

"Look," I say. "I shouldn't have reacted like that. I'm... I'm not in a very good place. And some stranger starts spouting stuff about me and I don't know what to do. Maybe this is all a joke someone put you up to, but I need it to stop. What do you say we start over? Tell me your name and how you know me."

He shakes his head. "Oh no you don't. I'll call the manager out here and see why a perfect stranger wants to know my name."

I chuckle. "I deserved that, didn't I?"

"Yes, you did.

"Steven," he says, "would it help if you knew that I'm from this neighborhood? I grew up here too. I remember when this place was Petrazello's. Gracious Sister of Monrovia, they had great pizza! The sauce... It had this sweetness to it. Remember? Nobody was sure if it was cinnamon or what."

"I'd forgotten that."

"You can't find that sauce anymore. It died with old man Petrazello."

Then he smiles warmly, searching my eyes. "Maybe it would help if I told you that I know your dad."

"You do? Why didn't you say that at the start?"

"I've seen you before this," he says. "You were sitting in the parking lot."

"How did you know it was me?"

"Your dad told me about the car. Steven, I don't know if you've noticed, but there aren't a lot of late-model SL-Class Mercedes in this neighborhood."

"So you know my dad, huh?"

He nods. "We were pretty good friends when you were a little kid. Hung out here a lot. Then I got on the fast track, and we sort of lost touch until a few years ago. Anyway, he brags about you, you know. So I've kind of kept a watch for you and followed your life the last couple years. That's how I was sure it was you today when you walked into Fenton's. I was walking out of Radio Shack next door and thought, *How cool is this? I know this kid, but he doesn't know me. Let's have some fun.*"

"So that's how you knew about Manhattan Beach?"

"Yep."

"So, you're not a mind reader, after all?"

"Not really. But I kind of was there for a while, wasn't I?"

"Yes, you were."

"I'm surprised he hasn't told you about me."

"Me too."

We're quiet again, both staring at the television set. Finally I laugh. "So are you going to tell my dad I threatened to beat up one of his friends?"

"No, that can be our secret."

"Explain this, then." I look away from the TV. "You said some things a couple minutes ago that my dad wouldn't have known. What was that about?"

He gives me a sideways look. "What stuff was that?"

"You know, the fight with my wife and...that whole bumping-into-furniture thing."

"Oh, I just get those little sayings off the Internet. Sometimes they're from Dr. Phil, sometimes Oprah."

"No, you don't." I shake my head. "How did you know those things about *me*? I hide that stuff pretty well."

"Maybe not as well as you think." He lets that last statement hang in the air for a while. I'm not sure what to say. This guy may be my dad's friend, but he's still pretty annoying.

He spins around on his stool and jumps up, like a little kid.

"Come outside for a second? I wanna show you something."

He takes a few steps toward the door and turns to me. "Come on, it's not like you'll miss your drink."

So I follow his flip-flopping feet out to the parking lot. There, sitting directly next to my car, is a shiny cherry-red vintage convertible.

He leans against the trunk. "Nice, huh? Buick Electra—1970. Only about six thousand ever made it to the street. Less than two hundred still running. Four-fifty-five with eight cylinders and 370 horses pulling this sled. I redid the whole thing myself from the ground up." He looks lovingly at the car. "Even the upholstery. The door panels and the whole steering assembly came from an Electra owned by Cary Grant."

When he sees my blank stare, he says, "He was an actor…in the forties and fifties, um, before Brad Pitt was born. Anyway, you gotta jiggle the passenger door handle from the inside to get in, and she drinks a lot of oil. But if you want to get your hair scared, there ain't nothing like this ride! You can sit in it if you'd like."

It truly is an impressive vehicle, especially the storage compartment which makes up half its size. You could drive a present-day hybrid into that trunk and still have room for groceries. This car looks like a shiny safety-deposit box on whitewall tires. No big fins, no gimmicks—Detroit's last attempt to build a car that could comfortably fill an entire lane.

I shake my head. "Thanks. I can see it just fine from here."

He hops in the car, starts the engine, and puts it in gear. "Suit yourself. Maybe we'll see each other again. Nice to meet you, though."

"Hold on a minute," I yell.

He puts the car back in park and lets the engine idle. "Look, Steven, you'll never discover most of what you went searching for tonight as long as *you're* setting the terms. That's how this stuff works. Maybe you came here for a reason. Or maybe you were brought here." He peers into my eyes. "What if God brought you here to meet an old guy with a Buick Electra who may be just a little further down the road than you? I don't believe much in coincidence. Maybe this is nothing more than a funny practical joke God let us stumble into. Or maybe both of us have been led here."

He reaches into his wallet and fumbles around.

"My name's Andy. Here's my card."

I take it from him. There's nothing on it but a name—Andy Monroe—and e-mail address.

"You decide you want to ride around in this cream puff, e-mail me. Okay?"

He puts the car into reverse. Then he smiles at me and slips on a pair of sunglasses as if it were noon.

His giant Buick Electra with white upholstery and white-wall tires slowly rumbles its way out of the parking lot. By the time I look up from putting his card in my wallet, he's vanished down Colorado Boulevard into the chilly early spring night air.

# "You Really Don't Get It, Do You?"

*(Late Evening, Wednesday, March 11)*

By the time I work my way down the Coast Highway and into our gated Manhattan Beach neighborhood, it's after eleven. Our gaslight-lined street looks even more quiet, safe, and elegant after driving through the area of sketchy, weed-choked rental houses that dominate life around Fenton's.

I pull into our circular driveway and turn off the car, admiring our home. The landscapers did a good job this week upgrading our ground lighting. This is the first time I've seen it at night. It really takes the shadows out of the front terrace and ties it in well with the surrounding trees and shrubs.

Lights are all still on inside. That's not good. It means Lindsey's up, probably rehearsing tonight's version of her disappointment.

*I don't need this. Not tonight.*

I sit there a while longer; tapping my fingers on the dash, hoping the lights will turn off.

*We weren't always like this. It wasn't this hard. I actually used to look forward to coming home. We'd call each other during the day. And when I walked in, I don't know, it was fun. I'd open some wine and we'd talk.*

More tapping.

*And what does she have to be disappointed about? What am I not doing? I could be doing a lot of other things than working this hard. If anyone should be complaining, it's me.*

Ten minutes later I finally walk into the house. Lindsey's standing at the kitchen sink and doesn't turn around at my "Hey there!" My wife is a strikingly attractive woman. She has dark brown eyes and hair exactly the same color. She's in great shape and dresses like she knows it. I married her, in part, because of her self-confidence. When we get crossways, it's what I can't stand about her.

"I've called three times today at your office and twice on your cell phone." She blurts it out with her back to me, like she's hoping the suddenness will cause me to confess something.

"Steven, you were going to pick her up from school today. You and her. You were going to have some time with your daughter. Remember?"

"Crap!" I start for the stairs. "I totally spaced it."

She lets me get halfway up before she says, "She's asleep. Come back down the stairs. You'll wake her up."

She turns fully toward me and lets me see her disdain.

"Steven, she stood at the loading zone for over an hour after school. Parents picking up kids circled around, concerned about her. 'Are you okay? Do you need a ride?' 'No,' she had to say over and over. 'My dad will be here soon.' "

"Enough. I get it." If I don't stop her, she'll just keep at me.

"She's eleven once," she continues. "This is it; this is that time. When you promise something, you can't just—"

"Don't start this," I say. "I made a mistake. I forgot. I screwed up, okay? I'll talk to her later."

"Oh, 'later.'" She nods sarcastically. "Which 'later' would that be, Steven?"

"Don't patronize me, Lindsey. You know what I mean."

"No, I don't. I really don't," she says as she paces into the living room, straightening magazines that are already straight. "Is this the 'later' like those other commitments you make and don't keep? Or is this a different one? I'm curious."

"Knock it off," I say, raising my voice. "I don't need this right now."

"Shhh! You're going to wake her up. She doesn't need to hear this."

"Oh, that's great," I say even louder, throwing my brief-case down. "Yeah, that's good. Take a few jabs and then tell me to be quiet. Great!"

She turns away and almost under her breath says, "I can't keep doing this."

"Doing what?"

"This." She swipes her arm across the entire room. "All of it." She holds her gesture, then slumps her shoulders and sighs. "I can't keep covering for you, Steven. Jennifer loves you. You're her dad. But she's starting to not trust you, to no longer count on you. I don't want that. I don't want my daughter to grow up that way. She deserves more, Steven."

"Don't start the drama, Lindsey."

"You don't get it, do you, Steven? The pattern doesn't change. You're upset with your life and you take it out on me, on us. I am continually walking on eggshells around you. I've never walked on eggshells with anyone. Didn't even know what it meant. And now, for Jennifer's sake, it feels like all I do when you're around."

She stops for a moment, as though she's counting the cost of what's coming next.

"You know what? I'm not unhappy—not until you come in with your resentment."

"Here we go," I mumble.

"You're so dissatisfied with your own life," she says, back to straightening things, "that you can't bear the thought of anyone being dissatisfied with theirs. You can't tolerate the notion that it could possibly have anything to do with you. So you tear into everyone and everything and can't understand why everything is all torn up around you."

"That's not fair," I shoot back.

"You're right. It's not fair. Here's how it goes."

She runs up to the front door, acting out what she is saying. "You walk in with something you're unhappy about." She runs back to the couch. "Then I try to reason with you. And you get louder and louder and meaner and meaner." She takes a step toward the kitchen. "Then, when I can't stand it, or you scare me enough, I leave the room." She then walks back into the middle of the living room with her arms stretched out. "And somehow you imagine that you won."

I try to respond, but she stops me, raising her hand.

"You know what?" She slowly shakes her head, a forced smile on her face that is more of a grimace. "I used to be able to stay in the ring with you. But something inside me has gone away. I've lost my confidence. I've lost who I used to be. I don't even recognize me anymore. So, Steven, you win. You've beaten me down to where I can't help you anymore."

"Look," I say, trying to calm myself down. "I don't know what you're talking about. I screwed up. Okay?" I walk into the living room. "Is that what you need to hear? I screwed up. I'll make it up to her. I can find some time later this week. I'm sorry, all right?"

She slowly walks over to stand right in front of me. "No, see, that's not going to work this time, Steven. I'm done. I sat here tonight, as I waited and waited... again. And somewhere around eight thirty I found myself thinking something's wrong with you. And I don't know what it is. I don't know if you're having an affair or if the man I thought I knew has turned out to be a phony. So I'm done. I mean, really done."

"Why do you do that?" I ask. I hate it when she pulls the "affair" card. "Why do you always have to accuse me of an affair? You do this all the time. You know you can get me angry accusing me of an affair. All right, you got me. I'm angry."

She spins completely around in exasperation. "You really don't get it, do you? You're so wrapped up in your own arrogant little world that you can't see what's going on, can you?"

"*My* little world?" I yell, getting louder with each word. "Oh! Excuse me, then. Would that be the arrogant little world that lets you spend half your day at a health club or gossiping with your little friends at fashionable little wine bars, on my dime? Would it be that arrogant little world?"

"See, there you go. You think it's all about the stuff. You think everyone should walk around bowing to you for what you can do."

She runs into the kitchen, calling out from there: "You're so blind, Steven. Jennifer isn't going to remember that she had all the stuff."

She walks purposefully back out of the kitchen, dramatically waiting a moment before she says: "She's going to remember that you weren't here. And even when you were here, you weren't here. That's what she'll remember."

"That's crap, Lindsey!" I yell.

"All we have ever wanted was you, your person. And with all your skills and magic, you have been totally incapable of providing that for your wife and daughter."

"Shut up, Lindsey. Shut up!"

"You're doing it again. You get angry, then you get loud,

and then you get stupid. Angry and stupid. Angry and stu-*pid*." She pops the *p*.

"Don't do that!" I step toward her.

"Do what?"

"Stop it! You know what I'm talking about."

"Do you know that what you find significant means nothing to either of us? All your importance at the office, all your greatness. Nothing. Zip. Nada."

That's when I snap. I yell and grab a vase of flowers off the dining room table, whacking her arm with my shoulder as I reach for it. I swing the vase like a discus thrower, flowers and water flying across the room and onto her. Then the vase slips out of my hands and explodes on the staircase. For a moment, we both look at the room, covered with flowers, broken glass, and dripping water. I'm breathing hard, my fists clenched at my sides.

"Sometimes," I growl through my teeth, "I really, really do not like you, Lindsey!"

She swallows. "You're acting like a crazy man, Steven." Her voice is forced calm.

I step right in front of her and yell at the top of my lungs, "Just shut up! Shut your stinking, stupid, fat mouth!"

She tries to move away from me. Almost involuntarily I block her path.

"Get away from me," she says quietly.

"No! I hate this!" My entire body is screaming. I can't calm down. "Do you hear me? I hate you! Do you hear me?"

Lindsey runs up the stairs. I run up after her, not knowing why. She's standing in front of the closet when I get to the bedroom.

"Get away!" she screams. "Get away from me, Steven! I'll call the police!"

"Stop it!" I yell. "Just talk to me. I'm not doing anything. I'm not going to do anything."

She runs toward the bathroom.

"Don't go in there, Lindsey!" I scream out. "I'm warning you. Don't close—"

Before she can close the door, I run toward it and slam my full weight into it. The door flies open, knocking her down on the other side.

She shrieks, "Oh, God! You broke my nose! I think my nose is broken! Get away from this door. Get away from me!"

I let go of the door. She slams and locks it. She's crying, moaning, and screaming all at the same time.

*What am I doing?*

"Okay. Lindsey, calm down. I want us to talk."

She's sobbing on the other side of the door. "I'm scared, Steven. I just need you to leave me alone."

"I didn't do anything."

"You hurt me! I'm bleeding."

I rest my forehead on the door. She's still sobbing. "Come on, Lin. That was an accident. I'm sorry. Open the door."

After a few moments she says quietly, "Steven?" She has stopped crying.

"What?"

She waits several more seconds before slowly saying, "I need to take Jennifer and leave right now."

"What do you mean? Leave where? Where are you going to go?"

"To my mom's. I need you to get away from the door and go downstairs. Will you do that?"

I hate everything about this. If she leaves, everything is going to go nuts. But I can't stop her. She's already scared.

"Are you really bleeding, Lindsey? Are you all right?"

"I'll be all right if you just get away from the door."

"All right, Lindsey. I'll go downstairs. I'm going downstairs right now."

I turn and in a blur somehow find my way down the stairs and to a chair at the far end of the living room. I sit there stunned, my entire body shaking. My mind is racing. *How did this happen? I've got to fix this and I don't know how. What is Jennifer going through? She had to hear most of that. What is Lindsey saying to her?*

In a few minutes both Lindsey and Jennifer descend the stairs, each carrying an overnight bag.

"Call me when you get to your mom's house, will you?"

Lindsey doesn't answer. Jennifer looks back at me, confusion in her eyes. She walks a step toward me and tries to say something, but nothing comes. Then she notices the broken vase and scattered flowers, evidence of what she just heard from her room. She turns back to me with a look of fear.

"It's all right, honey. Your mom and dad are just working through some things right now. Everything's—everything's going to be fine. I'll see you tomorrow. We all just need to get some sleep. We're gonna be fine."

There are no responses. Only the sound of the front door closing behind them.

# "She's a Lot of Detroit Magic, She Is."

*(Thursday Morning, March 12)*

Next time I check, my watch reads 3:00 a.m. I've spent the last few hours staring at the ceiling, rehearsing everything Lindsey and I said, replaying the scene of my wife and daughter walking out the door. I'm spent. I cleaned up the mess. Now I can't go to sleep, but I can't think clearly either. Lindsey never called from her mom's. I can't call her this late, so I have to wait a few hours to make sense of anything.

Everything's too quiet here in the dark. My head is buzzing. And for the last hour all I've been able to hear is Andy's voice from earlier in the evening: *"You could go back to what you've been doing.... But you'll be back.... And until you let someone shine a light into your room, nothing's gonna change. Life's gonna get more painful, more confusing and darker."*

Last night at Fenton's seems like a month ago now. Was Andy legit? Does the guy know my dad or is he just some spooky old stalker guy?

I grab my wallet to find his card.

*Let's just see what Google has to say about you, Mr. Andy Monroe.*

I sit down at the computer and type in "Andy Monroe." There's a songwriter named Andy Monroe. He dominates most of the first few pages. I'm pretty sure that's not him. There's also a playwright... an expedition diver... and a bull rider.

On page eight I find an article. "Langston Group: Andy Monroe Leaves Position as Financial Head." It's from 2003 and describes an apparently hugely successful forty-eight-year-old stepping away from his position at the request of the corporation for reasons of "personal indiscretion."

*Well, well, well. Is that you, Andy boy?*

He had said something that night about once being on the fast track. Tracks don't get much faster than the Langston Group. Those guys had dominated the South Coast financial scene since I was a boy. So maybe our flip-flop-wearing friend was somebody at one time, until "personal indiscretion" got the better of him.

*Still, how does a guy like this know my dad?*

I think about calling him, but quickly realize I'd rather not have him asking questions. Best not to mention it.

Instead, I nose around some more and start picking up repeat articles with the occasional grainy photo of a younger-looking Andy Monroe. Various entries detail Andy's exploits in the financial world, but everything just sort of stops with that "indiscretion" back in 2003. It's as if the Andy Monroe of the financial world ceased to exist after that. And I can't find a thing that ties him to Culver City or my dad.

I decide to pull down some boxes of family pictures from the garage. If this guy's for real, there has to be some evidence of it somewhere in my life. Besides, I got nothing else to do. Where am I going?

I make a pot of coffee, and within minutes I'm sitting at the kitchen table with pictures spread out in front of me. I almost forget what I'm looking for. It's been so long since I've seen pictures of my childhood. I'm actually almost enjoying myself. But there's nothing of Andy. Forty-five minutes later I begin refilling shoeboxes with pictures.

That's when I notice it—a picture of my dad and me on a

fishing trip. I can't be more than eight years old. Dad used to take me on those half-day chartered fishing trips off San Pedro. We'd go with his buddies—three or four guys who show up in a lot of our pictures. We really didn't know their families that well. They were just normal guys who grew up together in the neighborhood and never left. They all did guy stuff together: bowling, fishing, sitting around playing cards at Petrazello's. There was a heavyset bearded guy; Stan, I think. He was a machinist or something like that. I just remember his big, beefy hands always had grease in the cracks. There was Mr. Ketchum. He was a salesman of something or other. He and his wife did a lot of stuff with my parents. I really couldn't remember much about the others.

In the picture, I'm holding a fish that is several feet long. My dad has his arm around me. He's smiling. And behind us are the boys: Stan; Mr. Ketchum, a real tall guy wearing a straight-billed ball cap with a marlin on it. And *him*—Andy. He's younger and thinner, but it's clearly him.

He's smiling that same obnoxious grin, saying, *That's right, kid. It's me, Andy. You thought I was making it all up didn't you? You know, I actually helped you bring in this little trophy fish, my friend. I'm in several others too.*

I sit there stunned. This guy's a part of my family history, and I have no memory of him. I laugh out loud. *I almost decked a friend of our family.*

I decide to e-mail him.

Andy,

So, my wife and I, last night, we sort of got into an argument. Bottom line, I think maybe I could probably use a drive around to air some things out. Sorry again for how I reacted.

Steven Kerner

Within an hour, at 5:20 a.m., I get his reply.

Steven,

She's a lot of Detroit magic, she is. Couldn't shake thinking about her, could you?

Before you agree, there are a few things you should know:

1. I smoke cigars. Really good cigars. Never inside, but when I'm out in the Electra, I smoke. I'm not proud of it. But there it is.
2. Sometimes I play music while I'm driving. Sometimes I play it really loud. So, there's that.
3. We don't talk about the Los Angeles Rams' move to St. Louis. It's still a sore subject.

What do you say we meet at Fenton's next Tuesday, around 7:00 p.m.?

Andy

*That's it? Did this guy not get my e-mail? Next Tuesday? That's five days from now! And he makes no mention of anything I said. He's kidding, right?... No wonder my dad stopped hanging around with him.*

# The Marriott, Room 643

*(Midmorning, Thursday, March 12)*

By eight thirty Lindsey and I are on the phone with each other. She informs me that Jennifer needs to be in her home and that I should be the one who finds a place to stay. This isn't blowing over. I work until noon and then leave the office with an excuse, spending the rest of the day locating a hotel between our home and my office in Santa Monica. I end up at a Marriott in the business section of El Segundo. I drive back home to pick up some clothes. As I open the front door everything feels very odd, as if my own home is no longer even sure I should be here. This whole thing feels so humiliating. What am I doing, in the middle of a workday, packing toothpaste and business clothes to stay somewhere a few miles away? I change into jeans and a sweater. Before I walk back out the front door I hesitate, wondering what I'm giving up once I give in to this.

It feels like almost everyone is aware of my situation. Our next-door neighbor, Melanie Patton, an overweight woman in a perpetual hairnet, is out front watering bushes as I walk from the house carrying my hang-up bag. She's never liked me. I think her fashion sense brings property values down. She peeks over her sunglasses at me and turns away, like she's thinking, *Finally.*

The guy at the Marriott front desk stares at my driver's license. "Why, you can't live five miles from here." I give a weak nod, saying nothing. He looks at my bag, back at me, and then back at my bag again. He gives an awkward smile, as if he suddenly realizes he may have stumbled into a guy hiding from the law or something. Snatching up my license, a pen, and a room agreement, he drops them onto the counter, all in one noisy and flustered motion. I mumble something about relatives in town and scrawl out my name on the contract, all while moving away from the counter to the elevator.

I soon discover that a Marriott room at a resort destination and a Marriott room at a business park are two different animals. Mine has a bed, a "workstation," a smaller television, and a view of the top floor of a parking garage. It'll do. I'm not going to be here long. I open a can of nuts from the minibar, kick off my shoes, and flop back against the bed headboard, soon staring at an oil painting of a bowl of fruit. *Very edgy, Mr. Marriott. Very edgy.*

I'm not calling her. She'll call me when she feels bad enough, realizing I'm taking the hit for all this. I grab the channel changer and mindlessly surf cable stations, eventually lying in the dark, fighting this nagging thought that I should probably get up, put on some shoes, and walk down the hall for a bucket of ice. But I'm too drained to do anything about it. I think those were my last thoughts as I fell asleep to the sounds of the Food Channel, a half-eaten can of mixed nuts sitting on my chest.

# The Bluff Facing South

*(Tuesday Evening, March 17)*

Day six. I'm still sleeping at the Marriott. I've talked twice to Lindsey. All business and very cryptic. She did say, "I just need some time, Steven. I'll call you and we can talk about what comes next." I've stopped by the house several times when they're gone, to pick up mail and more clothes. I've talked to Jennifer on the phone once. She seems to be acting like I'm away on business, pretending nothing is very wrong or abnormal. She gets that from me, I think.

I'm discovering I hate eating dinner by myself. The worst part is, you run out of places to look. I need to take a book with me. I used to make fun of those nerds who read in public. Now, I'm wondering what they're reading. And everyone seems to be staring and talking about you, like they're warning their children, "Bobby, if you don't pay attention in school, you could end up like that man—all alone."

I've chosen to tell no one about what has happened. Nobody needs to know, and I'm pretty sure this won't last much longer.

He's sitting in the Electra as I drive up. I park my Mercedes at the end of the lot. This is the kind of place where some-one would open his door into yours without thinking twice about it. I get out, hit the Lock button on the remote, and walk toward his car. I pause at the passenger door of the Electra.

"Hop in. You'll have to reach in and use the inside handle."

He's wearing another gaudy Hawaiian shirt and the same Dodger's ball cap from the last time I saw him. I have the feeling his wardrobe has definite limitations. He puts on his sunglasses and leans over the passenger seat to hand me a pair. "You'll need these."

"These" are a clunky pair of black frames with equally black lenses. How anyone is supposed to see through these during the day, let alone at night, is beyond me.

"No, thanks. I'm good," I say, but he presses the glasses toward me with a look that says he won't take no for an answer. To move things along, I put them on.

As I look at Andy's self-satisfied grin, I'm having second thoughts about this trip. I'm not a very good passenger. I drive; I don't ride. But, even this seems better than spending another evening sitting around in my Marriott cell, room number 643.

I so want to tell Andy that I'm onto him—that I know all about his business failings—if only so he'll stop with the wizard routine. But I decide to save my findings for later. I also decide he doesn't need to know I'm living on the street, until I see how this ride works out.

I open the passenger door with the inside handle and climb in. The car is huge. I feel like I'm sitting on an enormous, slippery, plastic tuck-'n'-roll couch. I slide to the back of the seat until my feet are almost no longer touching the floor mat. It appears that back in the day, they manufactured cars for only giants to drive.

As I'm looking around for a seat belt, he notices and says, "It's jammed into the seat somewhere. Good luck."

So here we are... two men wearing sunglasses after sunset, strapped into seat belts with no shoulder harnesses, rumbling down the boulevard in a vehicle designed before fuel economy was a gleam in a car designer's eyes. For a while we're just driving, neither of us speaking a word. The combination of the wind in my face and the deep hum of the Electra 455 is almost trancelike.

He yells above the engine, "Mind if I smoke?"

"Would it matter?"

"Probably not."

"I guess I'm fine, then."

With an obviously well-practiced skill, he pulls out an old Zippo lighter, and as the flame flickers in the wind, he lights up a cigar he calls a Padron 1924 Anniversario.

Eventually we pull onto the 405 for a few minutes and then up into the hills overlooking Marina del Rey and Venice and the Pacific Ocean. Andy parks the car on a bluff facing south. From there you can see most of the L.A. basin. After some time looking over the city, he takes a long draw on his cigar and blows an impressive smoke ring into the still night air.

"Steven, if this was 1972 and I was sitting here with the top down in this gem with a pretty high school girl, well, let's just say that the guy in the Chevy Nova next to me would be driving back down the hill in embarrassment."

"I wouldn't know, Andy," I say. "I wasn't born yet. I don't think my parents had even *met* in 1972."

Andy clutches his heart. "Ouch."

Looking over the city, it strikes me that I haven't sat like this in a long time. Just sitting and looking at a great view for no other reason than because it's there. I begin to relax a little.

Eventually he breaks the silence.

"So, Steven, what do you see from up here?"

"What do you mean?" I ask.

"I mean, what do you see when you look out over the city?"

"I see lights. Lots of lights."

Andy rolls his eyes at me a little. "That's it? Lots of lights?"

"Yeah. What are you getting at?"

"Tell me what you imagine is going on in some of those homes down there."

*I don't like this. I don't need this. I'm not up for wherever he thinks this is heading.*

"Go ahead," he presses. "Humor me. What's going on down there tonight in L.A.?"

"I don't know," I say. "Lots of stuff. Some good, some not so good."

He takes a minute before speaking again. His tone seems to change; his volume is lower, his pace a little slower, as if he's saying something he thinks is important.

"Yeah, lots of *stuff*. Husbands and wives fighting. Angry kids fuming in their rooms, resenting their parents' authority. Some of those lights are cars with sad and lonely kids inside, driving around, acting tough, looking for something... anything."

Andy closes his eyes and rubs them. "It starts young, doesn't it? They get hurt. Maybe they get hurt real bad early on. And if they're not careful, they learn something that takes a lifetime to unlearn. They learn to cover up, to protect themselves. They don't even know they're doing it at first. But later they can't stop it even when they want to.

"All those people down there, walking and driving around, confused—angry, hurt, wounded, afraid, resentful—they all have some things in common."

He stops speaking, as if he wants me to ask. I begrudgingly reply, "What's that?"

"Well," he says, after doffing his cigar into an oversize ashtray, "they've learned to protect themselves. Now they're adults and they're discovering this cruel secret: *they can't protect themselves.* In fact, the last person who can protect them is them."

I turn to look at him.

"They end up trusting only themselves," he continues. "And all of these people have others around who could help them see…if only they asked for help. But fear keeps them from asking. So everybody does an elaborate dance around each other. A guarded, well-intended conspiracy of silence surrounds almost every conversation. What isn't said is louder than what's spoken. Friends dance around friends for years, holding back truths that would set the other free. The memories of failed attempts, hurt feelings, and estranged relationships block light from entering the room."

Andy pauses before saying, "We're an entire population of people with spinach in our teeth—and no one to tell us."

He puts his hands behind his head, leaning back into the sofalike seat. "Every light down there represents a person. Every light tells a story. A lot of them are stories of what happens when we try to self-protect."

I need to change things up. I open the door and walk out several feet onto the bluff. It is so quiet I can hear my feet scuffing at the dirt. I turn back toward the car. "What do you mean, 'self-protect'?" I ask, knowing I risk another speech.

"Self-protection. You know, that guarded self-deception where we miss how we're really coming off because we're afraid to let anyone tell us."

"Give me an example."

"Well, some forms are pretty inconsequential. Like talking too long before allowing the other to respond. Or talking too close. *Man*, that one, whew!" He shudders a little. "But there are much harsher and more damaging expressions of self-protection."

Andy takes another long draw on his cigar, adjusting his rearview mirror.

"These are the people fully blind to the destruction they're causing or allowing. Like a homemaker too embarrassed to tell someone about the hidden pain in her marriage—that she's contemplating running away to escape it. She's convinced she has to live alone in her pain.

"Or a high school student trapped by porn but too ashamed to let anybody know. So day after day, he wraps himself in increasing darkness that will follow him into his marriage and contaminate the family he'll one day raise."

I'm slowly walking along the edge of the bluff, taking in the entire Southland as he speaks. Andy's voice is like a narrator's sound track, and my eyes are the camera capturing what I imagine might be happening at this very moment in the homes below.

"Or maybe it's a single guy, so desperate to be known but so afraid he's gonna be rejected that he overwhelms anyone who gets close. A salesman so full of arrogance that he hides his true self from those he longs to impress. A teacher, still scarred by something once done to her. And now she wears a facade of bland, empty politeness—leaving her unable to really reach her students.

"All these people. How many of them will ever get to see their abilities released? They keep slamming up against the same wall because there's no one to protect them in their weak areas. And they end up bitter and cynical."

I call back to the car, "We've got an entire department at

my company. Creative Development. They all have talent to burn, but they've always got some fatal flaw just waiting for a run-in with a supervisor."

"And this isn't even including all the lights that have been intentionally turned off. They're convinced if others can't see an issue, it might not exist. These are the most pitiful ones. They're being eaten alive in secret. It's the hiding that gives their issues power. That's how addictions gain their strength. And slowly, it begins to define their lives."

"You ever struggle with this kind of stuff, Andy?"

He slowly looks back at me. "Every one of us wrestles with something, Steven, something that threatens to take us down. God watches these scenes every night, all night. Every one. He's the only One who can see in the dark." He pauses a moment and I think about how long its been since I thought about God. "It breaks His heart long before the rest of us see the results."

I kick at the ground. "And this is supposed to encourage me?"

He looks directly at me. "I'm sorry. I'm talking a lot, aren't I?"

"Yes, you are."

"Steven, let me ask you a question. What do all these people need?"

I walk back from the ledge, taking off the ridiculous sunglasses. "That's kind of like asking a person who's lost his keys to tell you where he lost them, don't you think?"

He smiles and then laughs. "That's good."

We're both quiet for a bit. I'm wishing I'd worn a jacket. And I'm wishing we could find a way to wrap this up. This really isn't heading in a helpful direction. I guess I thought he saw something that night and might have some advice.

And he's a nice guy. But maybe that's it. As a friend of my dad's, I suppose I owed him this. But that's as far as this needs to go.

Andy's leaning against the driver's door, like he's settling in for another long dissertation on something or other. I'm about to tell him I need to get back, when he speaks in almost a whisper.

"So, Steven, why weren't you able to go home that afternoon last week?"

Here's my chance.

"Great question. What do you say we head back and figure that out another time? I appreciate what you're trying to do. I've just got to get going."

He seems embarrassed. "Oh! You want to head back. Well... sure." He inspects his cigar. "I'm not even halfway done with this puppy. You want to head back, huh? Down the hill....?"

"It's getting a little chilly, and—"

He immediately sits up and fumbles with his keys. "Yep. Back. That's what we'll do." He starts up the car and I climb back in and buckle up.

We sit there for a few moments with the car rumbling. He's looking forward, his hand still on the keys. Then, as though he's had a complete change of mind, he turns the car off, reworks his ball cap, and turns back toward me. He stares at me for an uncomfortably long time.

*Just start the car!* I'm thinking.

"You're not used to answering questions like that one, are you?"

I look back at him, trying to look sincere. "No, it's not that. I'm just... I need to get back."

"If this was working for you, it wouldn't seem that way. You're just done with this conversation, aren't you? Impatient? Don't patronize me, Steven. That's what's happening, right?"

"Yes, Andy," I say. "That's what's happening."

He winces and then smiles. "Don't mince words; speak your mind, Steven." Then suddenly he slaps his hand to his forehead. "You know, I completely forgot! What would you say if I told you I had a Dodgers warm-up jacket in the trunk?"

"I'd say you're trying to keep us from going back."

He smiles as he opens the driver's-side door and heads to the trunk. "It's a really nice jacket. Give me a second."

A few moments later I'm wearing a Dodgers warm-up. Not a flimsy Windbreaker, but one of those shiny heavy-weight flannel-lined ones relief pitchers wear in the bull pen. This guy is something. It's like he just wants to be with me.

"So?" he asks, as if he's just served me a fancy dinner and wants some feedback.

"It's fine. Plenty warm. Thanks."

"About my question—you gonna take a hack at it?"

"I'm sorry, Andy," I say. "What was the question again?"

"Why weren't you able to go home that afternoon last week?"

"Andy, did you even read my e-mail?"

"Yes."

"Did you not read the part about Lindsey and me having an argument? You're up here with me and you're talking about people down there. I'd like to help them. But I happen to be in the middle of a marriage that's having some problems at the moment."

"Tell me about it," he says.

"It was just stupid. I forgot to pick up our daughter. And Lindsey lit into me. It's like she waits until she's got the right ammo. And then she keeps poking until she gets me angry.

She knows she can do it anytime she wants. It got pretty ugly. I got exasperated and I lost my temper." That's all he needs to know. "I just need to stop letting her get to me, you know?"

"That's it?" he asks.

"Pretty much."

Andy shakes his head. "Because I gotta tell you, it doesn't sound like that's it. Married people get into arguments. And most married people get exasperated. Comes with the vows. But none of that sounds like bumping-into-furniture-in-the-dark kind of stuff."

"Look, I know what you're gonna say. I know what I need to do. It's just a matter of doing it. Yeah, I'm not tracking with the God thing. And if I was, I'd be able to face things better. I should make time. But I get busy. I need to just get away and get things back in order."

Andy's quiet.

"They've got a married couples class at our church. That would make her happy, and we probably wouldn't be at each other's throats. You know, just being around other couples."

"A spiritual kick in the pants, huh?"

I give a half smile. "Well, yeah. I mean, more than that. But..."

"And that'll solve it? You know, that'll keep you from continuing to show up in Fenton's parking lot?"

"Andy, you want to know the truth? At least half of this stuff is about her. She says it's about me and of course I can't win that one. I have to give in and promise to try harder or whatever. But I can fix my stuff. It's her I can't figure out."

"And you were kind of hoping maybe I might be that magic man with the silver bullet, huh?" he says.

"What are you saying, Andy?"

"I'm saying that you think you understand what your problems are. You don't need anyone's help; you just need better coffee. Listen, there's a great place in Hermosa Beach. High-octane. We'll get you some caffeine, and you can be on your way."

He starts the car.

"Hold on a minute. I don't get it. Why are we leaving?"

He speaks over the sound of the engine. "I think I'm trying too hard for something you don't want. Maybe *I'm* the one getting cold now."

This guy is a piece of work. "Andy, I don't get you."

"Look, Steven, like those people down there, you've been protecting yourself like this all your life."

"What are you talking about?" I ask. "How could you know that?"

"Here's the pattern. You go along the best you can... until every now and then, when some 'problem' slaps you in the face. You ignore it until the slapping gets too painful. Then you go to work on the symptoms. Maybe you get your wife to admit to her issues, or you take an extra day off here and there. You patch things up, maybe learn how to argue nicer. You read a book on dealing with your anger. All symptoms. Maybe you even fix something and think life will now be all better. The slapping seems less frequent for a while."

I sigh. "And...?"

"And eventually the pain returns," Andy continues. "Only now it starts to scare you because you realize that what you tried didn't work. And you don't know it yet, but this time, you can't get back to your day-to-day. That's when you end up at Fenton's. That's how you end up here."

I scowl at him. "Turn off the car."

He does.

"What are you saying? We're not supposed to work on our issues?"

Andy shakes his head. "No. I'm saying you *think* you're

doing that. But you're only swatting symptoms. You think because you know something is wrong, you have the ability to solve it. You've been doing this for as long as you can remember. And so far, every time, you've been wrong. And it's not your fault, but you're zero for the last several years, my boy. And sometimes, late at night, lying in bed, you get really scared. A can't-go-back-to-sleep scared. Because you suspect there are deeper issues—ones you don't have the foggiest idea about—much less how to solve."

Almost against my will, my face unclenches. I look Andy directly in the eyes.

"And on this particular assessment," he says, "you are 100 percent correct."

"Look," I say, trying to get past the uncomfortable truth he's just nailed. "I thought you wanted to help me."

"I can't. At least not on your terms. So, are you gonna stop trying to buy me off and answer my question, or am I buying you a pound of coffee and sending you on your way?"

"Stop the drama, Andy. What are you trying to get out of me?"

*"A way in."* He reaches over and taps my chest with his fingers. "Has anyone ever had access to the real you? You've managed to keep everyone at the surface level for a long time. If you want help, that's got to stop. Even *I'm* too busy for that."

I shake my head and sigh again. I do not get this guy.

Andy reaches toward the ignition switch. "Look, it's late. I've confused you enough. Let's call it a night."

"Wait," I say, holding out my hand. "Lindsey and I—she asked me to leave the house. I'm staying in a hotel."

Andy waits for a few seconds before he suddenly yells out, "Oh, man, I knew it! I was afraid of that."

"What?"

"I *knew* it."

"Don't give me that," I snap back. "Nobody knows."

"I did. I'm good; that's all I can say."

"Okay. Tell me, then. How did you know?"

"When you pulled into Fenton's tonight. The parking-garage tag on your rearview mirror. An executive gets a nice little card or something." He slaps his knee. "I could have been a detective, you know?"

"My parking tag?"

"Yeah. Well, that and the fact that you look like crap. I mean, no offense, but few wives would let their husbands leave the house looking like you do. Have you taken a look at your hair?"

Just when I'm ready to rip into him, I look over and he's smiling kindly at me. He says quietly, "Thanks, Steven. That took a lot of courage. And I'm sorry. I really am."

I settle back into my seat, my hands in the pockets of the jacket. "So now what?" I ask.

"Down in that city, millions of people are hiding stuff, presenting only what they think they can control. They carry around guilt or anger or bottled-up hurt and don't have any idea where to put it. It eats at them. It wakes them up at night. It sits in the passenger seat on long drives alone. It goes with them on vacation. It follows them into church and drowns out the message."

In the distance I hear the low roar of an airliner cruising past. The hum of traffic below sounds like the noisy generator keeping all the lights on.

*It's like the noise in my head,* I think. *I can't stop it. It's like it's only getting louder and tearing everything apart around me.*

The next thought brings back the chill. *It's been there so long, what if it only keeps getting worse?*

Andy interrupts. "What are you feeling, Steven?"

"That's just it. I don't know. I don't feel. Most the time, I just do what I've got to do and don't worry about emotions. I don't like where I'm at right now, but mainly because it seems like I should have been able to figure it out by now." I pause, debating whether to share the next part. "But I guess it's also that no one knows Steve Kerner, and if I died today, I'd be nauseated by what would be said at my funeral."

It's quiet... and uncomfortable. I want to rustle the jacket just to make some noise.

Andy lights another cigar. He puts his hand on my shoulder. "That, what you just said a moment ago? That was good. It was real. We can work with that."

He starts up the Electra and we head down the hill, back toward the lights and the stories of pain and hiding, one of which is my own. The smell of his cigar, the feel of the wind, and the engine noise is comforting. Andy slides a Van Morrison cassette into the tape player.

We catch the 405 and merge onto Washington before taking the several-mile stretch of surface streets back to Fenton's. It must be nine-thirty. I look at my watch for the first time: 11:55.

He lifts his cigar in my direction. "You want one next time? They smell a lot better if you're smoking one."

"No, thanks."

"Thought I'd ask." He pulls the car to a stop next to mine.

I look down at my hands, unsure what to say after our strange evening together, but feeling strangely relieved somehow. "Thanks, I guess."

"You gotta jiggle the handle to get it open. I keep meaning to get it fixed."

I get out of the car and head toward mine. As Andy starts

to pull away, I turn back and flag him down. I walk up to the driver's side. "So, why are you doing this?" I ask.

"Um—" He scratches his chin like he's contemplating the answer to a riddle. "Because I can't get home without leaving the parking lot?"

"Why are you doing this for me?"

"Hey, can you get off some afternoon next week?"

"During the day?" I ask.

"Yeah, that's where they've started putting the afternoons now."

"You haven't answered my question."

"Right. Fair question. Lots of answers. Can we get at it next time?"

"Do I have a choice?"

"Probably not."

"Then I guess it's fine."

"Would you like my phone number, Steven? Just in case you can't make it."

"Okay."

I punch his number into my phone.

"It's a new phone. I'm not very good at answering it yet. I'm still trying to figure it out. Half the time it rings this obnoxious jingle; the rest of the time it doesn't ring at all. I'll find missed calls from the week before. But I've noticed it takes good pictures. Lot of money a month for a tiny camera. I actually tried to punch my number into my own phone yesterday. I wasn't made for this decade, I tell you."

"Yeah." I finish pressing buttons and pocket my phone. "I understand," I say, not understanding at all.

"Have a good night, Steven. How's next Thursday, say noon?"

I nod and he revs the engine and the giant Buick Electra rumbles out of the parking lot.

* * *

I check my e-mail upon my arrival back at the Marriott. Lindsey has written this:

> Steven, I've been praying a lot about this. I know this doesn't sound right coming in an e-mail, but I'm considering pursuing a legal separation. One moment I'm thinking I should call this off and invite you back home. The next moment I'm replaying one of the dozens of times where you yelled me down until I had to leave the room. Time apart and some talks with friends have opened my eyes. This is not normal, Steven. I don't want to live like this anymore. I love you, but I don't love this life we're in. I want Jennifer to have a future where she can just be a kid and laugh and hear laughter in her home. I don't know what needs to happen for you. You are so angry and unhappy and I don't know how to help you anymore. I've been thinking maybe going to church could have helped us; I just don't know.

# "My Respect for Burglars Is Rising by the Moment."

*(Friday Afternoon, March 20)*

I need a document on my desk at home for a meeting later today and I'm running short on clothes. So I leave the office and run over to our house at lunchtime. I put my key into the lock and the door doesn't open. I check my key and try it again. Nothing. I go around back and try the patio entrance. Same nothing.

*You gotta be kidding me. She's had the locks changed. Lindsey's locked me out of my own house!*

I stay in the backyard for fear that Melanie Patton might see me.

I call Lindsey's cell phone. I can't believe she'd do this. No answer. I check some doors. No luck. This is as stupid as it gets. Does she have a spare key under something? I'm so angry I can't even remember if we kept one outside for the old locks. Does a neighbor have a key? I call her cell phone again. I leave a message for her to call me. Then I try the garage side door. Locked.

Finally I discover an unlocked window. Jennifer's bathroom. It's tiny and about seven feet up. After several efforts of gouging it with a garden trowel, I eventually pry the screen off. I grab a lawn chair, prop it against the patio wall, and start to work my way up and over. But there's nothing below in the bathroom to break my fall. And the window's so small there's no room to cram my feet in first, so I try to wedge my legs around the outside brickwork and work myself down the bathroom wall—my left hand almost supported by the toilet-roll dispenser with the slick metal lid. I've now got grease on the front of my shirt from the window frame. Great. The final drop is about four feet.

*I cannot believe I am doing this, breaking into my own home, dangling over some really hard tile.... My respect for burglars is rising by the moment.*

Blood rushing to my head, I finally drop to the floor, landing really hard on my shoulder. I get up, inspect myself for damage, and begin my search for clothes and work papers. Then my phone rings. It's her.

"Steven?"

"Yes. Lindsey, do you know where I am?"

"No."

"I'm in our house."

"You're in the house?"

"That's right."

"What are you doing in there? How did... I had the locks changed."

"I noticed. Lindsey, what in the hell are you doing, locking me out of my home?"

"Don't even start. What are *you* doing? How did you get in the house?"

"Jennifer's bathroom window was unlocked. This is crazy, Lindsey. This is my house. I cannot believe you did this."

"You need to get out of the house right now, Steven."

"How could you possibly think it was a good idea to change the locks? Huh?"

"Steven, you scared me. You scared us. Gloria told me I should change the locks until we figure things out. I don't know what to do right now."

I scream into the phone. "Gloria Creighton told you! Great. The voice of reason. She's an idiot! I can't believe this!"

"Please, get out of the house, Steven."

"Lindsey, did you ever think I might need some clothes at some point? I'm picking up clothes and some papers."

"I don't know who to call. I want you out of there."

"Stop saying that!" I yell.

"Stop yelling at me, Steven."

"You locked me out of my own house!"

Then I hear a click. She has hung up on me.

I walk into the living room and sit down in the same chair I sat in the night they both walked out the front door.

*What is happening? This is so stupidly out of control.*

I don't know what else to do. I remember I have Andy's number. I call him.

"Hello? Hello? Geez, I hate that jingle."

"Andy, it's Steven."

"The danged thing rang this time. I completely miss a bunch of calls earlier and this one gets through. I'm at the same place the whole time. Go figure."

I'm rethinking my choice to call him.

"I don't even know why I called, Andy."

"Well, I'm not sure how I answered. So we're even. What's up, Steven?"

"I'm so mad I can barely sit still," I say. I'm up and pacing now as I talk.

"And so you called me? And to think I picked this one up and missed four others."

"I'm serious, Andy."

"So am I. I gotta get another provider. That's what they call 'em, right? Providers?"

"Yes, Andy. Providers."

"So, what's up, young man?"

"My wife locked me out of my house."

"Hmmm. That sounds serious."

"Look, I've taken the high road for the last, what, nine days? And look what it's gotten me. I should've never left this house. This is my house. Right? This is crap. She's got a whole pack of people taking up for her. It's crap! I'm not going to let this happen. If she wants someone gone, it's gonna be her. I'll freeze her credit cards; I'll freeze the checking. I'm not gonna keep doing this."

The line's silent.

"Andy?"

"That's another thing. The line can just go dead on me. For no reason. Thought it just happened again. Obviously not. 'Cause I can hear you talking now clear as a bell."

"Did you hear me, Andy?"

"Yes, I heard you, Steven. So you're gonna freeze her credit cards, huh?"

"I just don't want to make Jennifer pay for this."

"This reminds me of a Henny Youngman joke," Andy says. "You ever hear of Henny Youngman, Steven?"

"I guess."

Andy continues, "So a guy walks into the bar and says, 'My wife's credit card just got stolen.' So, I ask him if he's going to shut down the account. He answers, 'I don't think so. He's spending less than she did.' Woo, that's funny!"

I do not get this guy at all.

"Anyhoo," he finishes, like a bad comedian. "So, what then, after you freeze the cards?"

"I don't know. I'm just sick of this."

"Steven, listen to me. I want you to gather up enough clothes and stuff to last for a while, and then I want you to walk out the door and lock it behind you."

"What? I'm really serious, Andy."

"So am I, Steven. You scared your wife. I have no idea what you did, but you really scared her. And she has no ability to stop you. Only this temporary fix. You have no idea how serious this is. Unless I'm wrong, you don't want to lose her. And you are this close to losing her—this close. And you don't want that, Steven. Listen, you don't know me well yet, but this one is about you, my friend. Now you can hang up on me and freeze all the accounts you want, but tonight the furniture will move again, and you won't be able to turn that light on again for a long time."

"She says she's considering getting a separation," I add.

"I believe that."

"So, how is this about me?"

"Because, Steven, you've been arrogant enough to think you know what the issues are and how to solve them. You've been blaming everyone around you. And they can't take it anymore. They're so devastated by you that they're locking you out.... Other than that, everything's just fine."

"Yeah, but I—"

"Walk out the door, Steven. I'm hanging up now. You can call me, if you want, once you get back to the office or your hotel. Good-bye, Steven."

"Good-bye, Andy."

I sit back down in the chair, exhausted. I can feel the pain of my fall through the window all over. My head is throbbing. I want to say, *I'm not gonna listen to his psychobabble. Why would I listen to that? He agrees with her. He's on her side.* But as I sit there, I see Andy's goofy face staring at me, saying, *"And until you let someone shine a light into your room, nothing's gonna change. Life's gonna get more painful, more confusing, and darker."*

And I find myself going upstairs, packing clothes into a suitcase, and walking back downstairs and out the door, locking it behind me.

# "Angry People Eat, Don't They?"

*(Late Morning, Thursday, March 26)*

It's now been fifteen days since I entered my home without the use of a bathroom window.

Following Andy's counsel, I have stayed away. Anything I needed beyond what I grabbed earlier, I've purchased. Lindsey has appreciated my efforts and said yesterday that she'd like to meet somewhere soon and talk. She sounded less intense. I've picked Jennifer up from school several times to have that time together I missed two weeks ago. Things seem to be getting better.

Back at the Marriott, I've trained housekeeping, through a series of daily notepad instructions and exorbitant tipping, to take care of my dry cleaning and leave a bowl of oranges on the counter each evening. I love oranges and probably worry I could get scurvy or something, living in a hotel. I'm also putting in a pretty consistent hour of weights almost every night in the exercise room downstairs, which is more than I was getting at home.

I gotta say, there's something I'll miss when I move out of hotel life. You make a mess and someone cleans it up. And they smile at you for the privilege of doing so. Nobody's on you about making the bed, and you can watch whatever you want on TV. And people are nice to you. Everywhere you go: "Hello, sir." "Nice day, isn't it, sir?" "You think the Lakers will beat the Spurs tonight, sir?" Nobody calls me "sir" at home.

Today I'm supposed to meet Andy again. I almost called it off. I'm feeling manipulated by him. His revving engine drowned out any chance for response the other night. I don't mind driving around in the evenings, but this is a workday. Monday through Friday is a nonstop blur of fifteen-minute meetings and cell messages. To top it off, I left the office yesterday feeling as if a coup is brewing between a couple of board members and our head of human resources, all aimed in my direction. I don't get Whitney. She's the head of HR, but she's far more effective as director of rallying the board against Steven. I need to get there before they convene any more private teleconferences.

Andy is already there when I pull up to Fenton's, sitting comfortably with his arm across the front seat of his car. He looks as if he slept in his clothes. I feel incredibly conspicuous in my suit. But I needed to wear it today for an earlier meeting. He's wearing those same dated sunglasses. I'm wearing my Oakleys, but he hands me a pair of thick, heavy, old-school shades. "About your sunglasses," he says. "Uh, how do I say this delicately? These might look better, don't you think?"

*I can't believe what I'm hearing.*

"Look," I shoot back. "These are top-of-the-line. Light as a feather. The best out there. Yours look like you found them under a pile of old clothes at a thrift store."

"Are you kidding?" He scrunches up his face in disbelief. "Who would throw away a pair of these babies? You'll never find a pair of Wayfarers at a thrift store, buddy. These are Ray-Bans, my friend. The genuine article. Bob Dylan's wearing these on the cover of *Highway 61*."

He hands them to me again and says, "Humor me."

I begrudgingly put on his twenty-pound sunglasses, and we're off.

This whole thing doesn't feel right. In daylight, this whole *whatever it is* feels really odd. I don't know if I'm frustrated with Andy's sunglasses issues or with having to cancel three meetings while he takes for granted that I will. I did appreciate our talk on the hill last week. It was good to get that all out. And as much as I wanted to choke him during that phone call from my house, what he told me was probably right. It sure seems to have worked with Lindsey. But it's time to end these therapy rides. I need to tell Andy enough to let him know he's in over his head. He already knows way more than I'm ready to let anyone into. I know how these things go. You let one person in on an issue, and the next moment you're sitting in a circle with a bunch of slugs still living at home, one of them saying, "What Steven needs is a giant hug!"

So I'll frighten the old guy a bit. Give him a few choice excerpts from the last fight with Lindsey. Then I can thank him for his concern and get back to my world.

"Andy, I've got real anger issues," I blurt out over the noise in the car.

He looks over at me and smiles. "Really? Now, see, I never would have guessed that. Anger, huh? Shoplifting, maybe, but anger you say. Boy, you think you know a guy."

I yell louder. "You're not taking me seriously!"

He glances over again. "You are aware you're yelling really loud, right?"

I kind of want to punch him at this point. "Are you hearing what I'm saying?"

"Yeah, I get it," he says. "You could go postal on me at any minute." Andy rests his hand on the steering wheel. "So what sounds good for lunch?"

"I mean it, Andy. Something is wrong. I explode at my wife, my associates, sometimes even my daughter, Jennifer. It's a real thing. I've done it for a long time."

"I believe you," he says. "Do you want to rage right now? I could pull over."

I look back at him blankly.

"Otherwise, I need lunch. What do you say we head out to one of my favorite places? They serve a shrimp cocktail that'll cure rickets. This is not conventional shrimp cocktail. This puppy's got huge purple onions, cucumbers, and big fresh shrimp. They serve it on a plate. *On a plate,* for crying out loud!"

"What is with you, Andy?"

"What's with *me*?" he asks. "I'm not the loud, angry guy."

He looks over long enough to see that I'm not smiling. Then slowly and clearly he says, "Steven, I understand that you have an anger issue. I get it. I understand it's a big deal. It hurts people you care about. I believe you. I also believe you don't have much confidence that I, or anyone else, can help you. And so you're playing it like a trump card so I won't get too close. You threw that out in hopes of ending our times together."

He continues looking ahead as he speaks. "Look, Steven, I have no desire to be your fixer. I want to be your friend. And friends learn to trust each other with their stuff so they can stand together. That and they borrow tools. So the more you can let me know the real Steven and the more I can let you know the real Andy, the sooner we can begin to sort things out. That's it. That's my angle. Period. I'm not scared off by your arrogance, your anger, or your rudeness. Now, you start ripping up my upholstery with a box cutter and that might freak me out a bit.

"If you want, we can turn this car around and be done with the whole thing. Or a guy with a real anger issue, sitting next to an equally flawed man, can go have some lunch. Angry people eat, don't they?"

I stare at the floorboard and sigh. "Yeah, angry people eat."

"Good," he says with a nod, and the Electra seems to pick up speed a little. "I'm telling you, it doesn't come in one of those little parfait cups. But on a *plate.*"

Once I resolve that I'm trapped, I actually find myself relaxing a little. I put my phone on vibrate and allow myself to calm down... as much as I can without a shoulder harness. I fold my arms and lean back against the Cary Grant upholstery. Behind the oversized sunglasses, I close my eyes and try to let the sound of the wind block out everything.

I must have nodded off for a few minutes because when I open my eyes Andy is parking the Electra across from what looks like some kind of impromptu street market.

*Where are we?*

Makeshift booths and little trailers with rolled-out cloth awnings line the street. The people inside are selling flowers, fruit, vegetables. It's like a throwback to an earlier era. Locals are out walking dogs, riding bicycles, and buying zucchini. It's like this market is giving the neighborhood an occasion to get out and introduce itself. It must be a regular thing because the people in the booths call out to customers as if they're old friends.

Andy's not saying a word. He's allowing me to figure out the scene for myself.

The folks look like working people, chatting, laughing, yelling loudly. A smiling guy in a flannel shirt heaves a crate of nectarines up onto a counter. Behind the counter, a woman with her hair covered in a bandanna and wearing dirty bib overalls and a very stained apron is chiding him about the quality of the fruit he brought her last week.

In the center of all the activity, a delivery truck is unloading fish into the side door of a restaurant. They're taking the occasion to make their fresh catches available to the locals. Two men are hauling huge, bloody cuts onto several nearby tables covered with newspaper. Two teenage girls are shouting, laughing, and throwing around what appears to be yellowtail tuna like bags of sand. The guy's daughters, I imagine. I think about Jenny. I can't picture the two of us slinging fish together. She'd never relax around me enough to keep from dropping them.

The smell of fish is heavy but not bad. It's kind of nice. Something real. I'm struck that not much of my life is like this. When was the last time I walked through a street market? When was the last time I walked around without my laptop on a Thursday afternoon?

Suddenly someone begins to yell in our direction from across the street. An immense, bearded, dark-skinned man is approaching us, and he's not smiling. "Andy Monroe! What the deal is? You bring the suit down here to audit us?" He's signing for the fish delivered into his restaurant.

"No!" Andy yells back. "You have to actually make money for someone to audit you. The suit's here to foreclose on you."

The immense bearded man leans back and laughs hard. "Git on in here now. Tell the suit lunch is on me."

Immediately we're ushered through the front doors of a seafood restaurant called Pacific Bayou, which Andy tells me everyone calls Bo's. The large man is Bo. He is as loud as he is intimidating. We're whisked through the dining room and out onto a patio, where several tables and some standing heaters sit on a deck.

Bo, with a firm grip on my arm, guides me to a nearby table. "Your friend, he sits right here at this table every Thursday, summer, winter, rain or shine. What the deal is with that? Don't ask me, *cher.* Git you a seat. You need a menu?"

But Andy's at my side again. "Bo, this is my friend Steven. He has an anger issue."

"Like I *don't*?" Bo says, fixing me with a devastating stare.

"We need a bucket of clams," Andy says. "I'll have the jambalaya and a glass of ice. My friend needs your shrimp cocktail."

"We got us none of dat," Bo bellows. "We got us carp. You git you some six-day-old carp, and you'll like it."

With that Bo disappears back into the restaurant, barking out orders, insults, and greetings in every direction.

"He says that almost every time, no matter what I order. One day I'm gonna order six-day-old carp and see what he does."

I shake my head a little. "The guy's pretty intimidating. I guess he's kidding, but he sure doesn't look like it."

"He's a pussycat, trust me," Andy says, grinning. "He came out here about twelve years ago from New Orleans with two thousand dollars and a headful of recipes. And he's done well."

"Yeah, Cajun was catching on about then. Who ever heard of the stuff before that? He caught a good wave apparently."

"Not just a wave," he says. "A guy like Bo will do well no matter what the current rage is. Sorry about the word *rage*," he mumbles under his breath. "I know it's a sensitive area for you."

I smile. "Good one," I say.

"But really," he continues, "he loves what he does and loves seeing people smile when they taste his food. He's the kind of guy who takes care of his customers. When you do the job for the love of it, it's hard to go wrong."

"So where does a name like Bo come from?" I ask.

"Bodinet LaCombe," a booming voice returns just behind my ear. I about jump out of my skin. Bo is there with a glass of water and a glass of ice. "Now who gonna go around with a name like *Bo-din-day*?" he says, mocking the pronunciation. "Not dis Creole!"

Bo disappears again and Andy leans in toward me. "Steven, a lot of my friends come here on Thursdays. Sort of a regularly scheduled meeting you don't have to show up for. So usually everybody does. I wanted to introduce you to some of my world. There's someone here I'd really like you to meet. The person who helped me through a lot."

Over the next fifteen minutes or so, the deck begins to fill with dozens of people who all seem to know Andy. The interactions are so fast and fun, I'm almost afraid to speak. Andy smiles and whispers, "Relax. Just be you. They're all mostly harmless."

I'm so overwhelmed at first that I fail to notice that the deck is in front of an ocean. And the restaurant marks the entrance to a pier. I suddenly know exactly where we are. This used to be my world. We're at Washington between Marina del Rey and Venice Beach. This cul-de-sac has been home to impromptu farmers markets all the way back to my childhood. There's nothing like this stretch. The pier has always separated Southern California wealth and opulence from maybe the most bizarre strand of post-hippie culture anywhere in the world.

*Wow! I haven't been here in a long time.*

As Andy works the deck, I replay memories of riding bikes down here with childhood friends.

My gaze is interrupted as I notice a striking and stylishly dressed middle-aged woman at the table next to me. She is beautiful in the way all women should be when they get to their fifties. Her hair is as wild as her colorfully flowing peasant dress. On both arms she wears a bundle of thin silver bracelets, which make light clinking sounds as she moves.

She isn't trying to hide the gray that has crept in, which makes her even more cool and beautiful. I want to take a picture and tell Lindsey, "Remember this. This is what you must look like twenty years from now."

*Maybe I'll wait on that for a bit.*

She looks so totally at peace and comfortable with herself in the midst of a noticeably younger crowd. She is tapping away at a laptop. She glances over and gives me a kind smile and nod. Andy notices my staring as he returns to the table.

"That's Cynthia. I wanted you to meet her first. She's working on a book. Something about first-generation immigrants in America."

"Working, as in laboring, as in plodding...," she adds, drifting effortlessly from her table to ours. "Forgive my rudeness, but I have a flair for overhearing conversations."

Andy stands. "Cynthia, this is—"

"Steven," she finishes without missing a beat.

*Great. Another mind reader.*

She reaches for my hand, her bracelets making that jingling sound. Cynthia looks as if she could be my sixty-two-year-old mother—if my mother were a lot hipper, flamboyant, and attractive.

Cynthia is at once incredibly disarming and overwhelming. She's one of those rare people who can sit too closely (as she is at this moment), without you minding much. She seems to be studying your eyes, reading your personal history while casually mulling among any of seven different thoughts that might come out of her mouth.

Andy interrupts. "I've got to wash up. I'll be back in a minute."

Suddenly the moment is broken. *What have I gotten myself into? I've got to get back to work.*

There is an awkward silence for a few moments. Cynthia is very content to just smile and stare at me.

"So you're writing a book?" I ask, mostly to stop the silence and the staring.

She rolls her eyes. "Ohh!" she says. "I'm never going to survive it."

"It's about immigrants?"

"Refugees, mostly. Dear, there are rather consistent characteristics to every people group that most easily adapt into a new culture. Did you know that?"

Before I can answer she continues, "Of course you didn't. That's why I'm writing the book, isn't it? Somehow I convinced the publisher there's a market." Her eyes twinkle a little. "Who knows? Maybe I'll get rich. More likely they'll make nice Christmas gifts. It's really just something I enjoy doing."

More silence...

"My dear, have you noticed you're not saying anything? One of the primary requisites for a conversation is the back-and-forth part. I can't do that on my own. I would if I could, as my husband will tell you. But right now you're going to have to step to the plate."

"Right," I mutter. "Sorry, I'm a little new here."

She laughs out loud and jumps up to smother me in a hug. "Well, if you aren't the most precious thing in the world. 'I'm a little new here.' Honey, that's like being a little engulfed in flames. No, you're completely and utterly new here. And in a ridiculously nice suit, I might add!"

She laughs some more. Then she sits back down, gathers herself, and looks into my eyes again with great sincerity. "Steven, you were new seconds ago. But now you've been willing to let a silly old woman laugh at you and hug you. From this moment on you are no longer new. You're a regular. Welcome to Bo's, young man." She hugs me again, jingling all over.

I mumble something back to her, but I am stunned. Less than an hour ago, I was trying to end the ride that brought me here. Now I'm taking in ocean air fused with the smell of shrimp and corn on the cob, smiling at this woman who is completely delighted at my awkwardness. She's staring again, contentedly waiting for me to catch up. I'm not used to catching up. I'm also not used to noticing the way the waves crash against pylons on the pier. But that's what I'm doing.

"Steven," she eventually calls out.

My eyes come back into focus. "I'm sorry, Cynthia. I grew up around here. I'm just taking it all in."

She pats my hand. "Forgive me, Steven. I can be a little much all at once. You don't know me and I don't know you. But my friend Andy...he cares about you. So now you're important to me. It's kind of that simple. I don't know if what I'm about to say will make any sense, but here goes."

She is sitting too close again as she says, "Don't miss what is being offered to you. It would be easy for you to miss it. You've got deadlines and quotas. When life is moving fast and in a straight line, it's easy to discount anything slow and circular."

"Miss what?" I ask.

"Forgive me again. I'm rushing ahead. It's just that I wanted to get this out while Andy wasn't at the table." Cynthia's smile and the way she puts her hand on my arm is reassuring.

"Let me back up a little," she says. "I was Andy's wife's best friend—"

"Excuse me," I interrupt. "*Was* Andy's wife's best friend?"

"My wife died, Steven," Andy answers as he returns to the table. He turns his chair backward and sits, his arms folded across its top. "She contracted a quick-moving form of cancer. She fought courageously, but the cancer won."

I blink once. Twice. "I'm sorry, Andy. How long ago did this happen?"

"It was about six years ago." He stops. His mouth starts moving like he's going to speak, but nothing comes out. He looks over at Cynthia.

I interrupt my own question. "We don't have to talk about this right now."

Andy continues as if I haven't spoken. "When Laura died, I was a mess. I drifted away from almost everyone. People reached out, but I just wanted to be alone. Somehow I managed the bills and continued to work. But I was walking around like I was wearing several heavy winter coats. Each day my goal was just to make it back home and to bed.

"One night, about four months after her death, I was alone in that big house where all our life had happened. I was just overcome with grief. Blackness. I heard a knock at the door. It was Cynthia and her husband, Keith. They had takeout from a favorite Mexican place where the four of us used to go."

Andy's words lock up again. Tears come into his eyes. After a few moments he sighs and is able to speak again.

"We all sat down, and I started pouring out how depressed I was and how much I missed Laura."

"Then *I* broke down," Cynthia adds. "Oh, honey, we were basket cases, the three of us."

Andy looks at me. "Steven, I didn't plan on bringing this up."

"No, go on. Please," I say. This is the first info I'm getting on Andy apart from what I found on the Internet.

"I told Cyn and Keith that Laura had been my strength. I was the successful one out in the world, but now I was completely undone without her.

"Cynthia began walking me through some painfully good stuff that night. In the middle of wrestling with her own grief, she took the risk to tell me some hard things about myself that I'd avoided for a long time."

"Wait," I say. "*Cynthia* is the friend you were talking about who helped you?"

"Yeah," he says, wiping his eyes. "She and Keith. But mostly Cyn."

Before I can stop my words I say, "I didn't think you were talking about a..."

"A woman?" the two of them say in unison, then laugh out loud.

I'm embarrassed, but I start laughing too.

"Oh, yes! A woman!" Cynthia says. She smiles at me—a smile that tells me she can see right through me and is fully prepared to enjoy me anyway.

At that moment two men appear and sprawl out at our table as though they've been there for days and just got up to use the restroom. One is a dark Hispanic man. Strikingly handsome, he has a big, beaming smile. He has on an old sport coat over a T-shirt tucked into jeans. He wears canvas shoes with no socks. Most can't get away with this look, but this guy doesn't really seem to care, which kind of makes it work. The other man is sturdy and bald with a forehead that could stop a truck. A linebacker's forehead. His clothes have the rumpled look of a refrigerator salesman who does his own deliveries. The Hispanic guy is bantering with almost everyone—part English, part Spanish slang. I have yet to make out much of what he's saying by the time they've settled in at our table. It's all motion, jargon, and fun.

The handsome one extends a hand. "My man! You must be Steven. I am Carlos Badillo, at your service. And the Cro-Magnon–looking gentleman to my right is Hank."

I'm half-tempted to look down to see if I'm wearing a name tag again. Carlos leans in, points at Hank, and under his breath warns, "Careful with him, man. He just got out from a stint in the slammer for a number of violent crimes against the elderly."

Hank grunts back without smiling. "I was innocent on most of them charges, I swear."

Carlos has thick jet-black hair, combed straight back. He looks to be thirty-something. Hank, easily ten years older than Carlos, appears fully capable of what his friend has accused him of. His piercing eyes and heftiness match his apparent intensity. He looks like a cage fighter on a lunch break.

"So talk," Hank commands, gesturing to me.

Carlos nods in agreement. "I'm with him, man. Spill."

They both sit there, staring at me, fiddling with packets of soup crackers as though they can't go on with their routine unless I give some kind of response.

Andy rescues me. "Steven, these are two of my close friends. We've been meeting here on Thursdays, at this table, for a long time now."

Like a kid, Carlos jabs me in the shoulder. "Hey, man, has he fed you the 'bumping into furniture' speech yet? It's one of our favorites."

Hank joins in. "Yeah, I love that one. Show him, Carlos. Show him. You do it best."

Sheepishly, Carlos stands. "You think so?"

Both Cynthia and Hank nod in agreement.

He shakes out his hands like he's about to perform a platform dive. "All right, this is my impersonation of Andy doing the 'bumping into furniture' speech." He clears his throat. " 'It's like you're stumbling around in a dark room, bumping into furniture.' " Carlos leans over to me. "Then he'll wait a few seconds, just to add drama, before he asks you—"

Carlos and Hank say in unison, "So how am I doing?"

With that, Carlos and Hank start slapping each other's hands, laughing and wheezing. Several people on the deck seem to be enjoying the bit as well.

*He* was *just guessing that night,* I think, unsure whether it makes me feel better or worse.

Almost involuntarily, I ask, "Has he ever used the 'pound of coffee' thing on any of you?"

Carlos moans. "No way, man! You're kidding me, right? He's used that on you? Andy, I'm hurt, dude! I thought that was only for me. What, man? You stealing this stuff off the Internet?"

"I *told* you I was," Andy protests.

More laughter rises from the deck.

The next several minutes are all aimed at Andy's expense. He doesn't even try to stop the barrage, laughing along at the ribbing. The waiters and busboys are joining in too. The deck is definitely out of control.

Sitting here amid the laughter, I realize I'm watching something pretty uncommon. It's obvious that everyone on this deck deeply respects Andy. Their humor seems more of a way of honoring him. It's very different from the kind of mocking humor at work. There's no hard, cynical edge. Nothing competitive. They aren't really ridiculing him at all. Quite the opposite, actually.

Not long after I down the last bites of a truly great shrimp cocktail, Andy, Cynthia, and Hank excuse themselves, promising to be back in a few minutes. I am left at the table with Carlos. He appears in no hurry to go anywhere.

"So, where do you think they've gone off to?" I ask.

"Hank, he sells drugs and munitions out of the back of his car," Carlos says, not looking up from his food. "I've tried to steer Andy right, but he can't resist. It's a deadly combination, man."

I laugh by myself. "So, Carlos, how long have you known Andy?"

"A few years now. Maybe five. We met down at the marina. I was checking out a place to keep this little boat I have. The place was way too expensive for this Mexican."

"He owns a boat?"

"No. He works there."

"Andy works at a dock?"

"Yeah. Just down the street, on Tahiti Way. Why?"

"Nothing, really. I guess I just thought that, well..."

He leans back. "That my man would have a more impressive career?"

"Well, yeah, maybe."

"Well, suit, you've stumbled into a long story. You in a hurry?"

"I was about a half hour ago," I say. "It's starting to look like today's going to be a wash at work. And Andy's driving, so until he gets back... you think you could stop calling me 'suit'?"

He chuckles. "I don't think so, but I'll try."

"Fair enough."

"You see the people around this deck?" he asks, leaning back in his chair to point at various people. "Most of them know each other. You got your doctors and lawyers. There's a sheet metal guy, a city council member, a couple of plumbers. Tech nerds chillin' with hospital workers. Shop owners, students from Loyola. See the woman in the purple top? She was on the Olympic volleyball team at Seoul. Now she runs a physical training center in Newport Beach." He turns back to the table. "See that? We've got, like, celebrities here, man. And then there's Hank. You wouldn't know it, but he's an environmental detective for the state attorney general." He laughs hard. "That single fact alone should keep you up at night."

"I think it will from now on," I say.

"So most of us have, like, at least a couple things in common: One, we can't live without Bo's cooking. Two, most of us believe in God, or at least aren't hating that the others do. It's all word of mouth. And your new friend Andy, he's kind of at the center of it. The whole shindig never probably would've happened without him. He's had a pretty stinkin' huge impact on a lot of lives."

"I'm starting to catch on to that."

Carlos slides his chair closer. "I think he figures most people don't have someone safe enough when things go south. So the dude kind of watches for people who might be discovering they need something like that."

"Kind of like me?" I ask.

Carlos ignores my question. "Everyone needs it. Everyone, man. Most just don't see it. He's always watching for it. May not seem like it. The cat sometimes seems like he's listening to music in some other town. He doesn't always seem..."

I try to help. "Focused?"

"Yeah, focused. Sometimes he seems to be answering questions nobody's asking. Other times he's not answering what you *did* ask. Right? That old dude drives me nuts sometimes. But don't let the clothes and the slouching fool you. The old dude is sharp. He's listening. I've figured out he's waiting."

"Waiting?"

"Yeah, he's waiting to hear if the person is ready to risk letting someone inside, past the show, past the dance."

"So the people on this deck—they're the ones who have let him in?"

"Yeah, sort of, but not all. I do it now too—listening. Cynthia does it. Even Hank. A bunch of us. We're all listening."

"You doing that with me right now, Carlos? Are you listening to see if I'm ready?"

He laughs so hard he leans back and hits his knee on the table. "Oh, no, man! You kidding me? Carlos can't be listening to everyone. Carlos loves to hear himself talk. I'll let Andy do the listening with you. Till they get back, you're stuck with me eating and talking. *Comprende?*"

"Yeah, Carlos, I'm good with that," I say. "So what does he do when he meets with you?"

"What do you mean?"

"Like, what does he talk about when you're together?"

"Hmmm." Carlos stares past me. "I don't know. I guess I don't think about it. We eat. We always seem to eat."

He motions to a busboy walking by. "Jorge, when you get time, *mi bebida con sucar. Gracias.*"

Carlos turns back to me. "Here's something. Maybe it'll help answer your question. Andy was the first dude I ever met who had more confidence in the grace of God than in the power of the crap I was dragging around."

I shake my head. "What?"

Carlos laughs. "Oh, yeah. Get your head around that one, amigo. It'll set you free. Steven, most people want to fix stuff in others so they don't keep embarrassing them no more. You know what I mean?" he says, smiling and nudging me. "It's true, man. It's like if they can't just get away from you, they're afraid of you stinking up the place. And that won't look so good for them."

I reply, almost to myself, "I don't think I've ever heard anyone say that before."

"You need to get out more. See, man, we want others to think we've got it all together, like we don't need a handout. So we stack the deck, we bluff, we cover up the stuff we don't like about ourselves. We make ourselves a nice little mask. And then we hide behind it. It's who we wish we could be, who we wish others thought we were. What a joke, huh?" Carlos shakes his head. "One of my masks was my position. I wouldn't have known then to say that. But I know it now."

"Your position?"

"I was the pastor of a big church in Covina." He sits up and puffs out his chest. "*El jefe. El camaron!* Lots of people looking up to Carlos, wanting to make me somebody bigger than life, like some kind of pope or something. Make me out to be this magic dude of faith...all squeaky clean and together and shiny. It's like you know better, but you start thinking to yourself, *Carlos is the man!* Yeeesh. I'd laugh if it wasn't so stinking stupid."

"You were a pastor?" I ask.

"Still am," he says. "Different church. Back then I had the badge, but I probably caused more damage than good. Or, well, you know, God had a plan, and in that part of the plan, Carlos Badillo was a pastor in Covina. Right?" He shrugs his shoulders and takes a big bite from the plate of fish he's working on.

"I met Andy before I started pastoring this church in Hermosa Beach. Go figure, huh? Me in Hermosa Beach. George Lopez hanging out with surfer dudes. I didn't have none of the lingo or nothing, man. Growing up, my people didn't show up at Hermosa Beach 'less they got lost."

He wipes his mouth with his napkin. "Anyway, Andy was the first person able to handle Carlos with all his junk. See, the dude was convinced that God in Carlos was enough. You gotta be kidding me, right? Really, man, that one thing, that someone saw me that way—it knocked me over. You know? For maybe the first time, like, ever, it gave me something strong to hold on to. Like there might be a way to face the lies tearing my insides apart."

He takes a quick drink from his water glass and continues, "And they were tearing me apart. Bad. Before then I didn't know how to just do each day without hiding or acting all big. Nobody knew me, not really. I'm smiling all the time like I'm in the know, like I'm in on the joke, you know? But the whole time Carlos is sitting on the outside wondering when people will see through him."

The busboy moves in, taking plates and refilling the water glasses. I'm noticing that Carlos is talking loud enough that people several tables away can easily overhear his confessions.

My voice instinctively drops. "So what happened? What changed?"

"Oh, man!" He slaps his knee and starts talking even louder than before. "I was the preacher guy. But I was a phony. I was a joke. I was standing in the pulpit week after week, all puffed up, all macho, talking all confident about God like I knew how to do life better than them. But I look back.... Yeeesh, I didn't know nothing. I was spouting clichés I heard from other people who didn't know nothing either."

Carlos mops up some of the sauce on his plate with a piece of sourdough bread. "I'd tell them all every week to be better, you know, 'be-worthy-and-walk-the-talk' kind of stuff. Real 'man up' power talk. But it was just loud words and fake authority. I didn't know how to help anyone be anything—except some fake dude like me, some dressed-up pigeon strutting around."

He bites off a hunk of bread, chews, and holds out his hand as if to hold me off.

"But then one morning, right in the middle of my ranting, I look down and see the people in my audience. For maybe the first time I really look at them. I'm just staring. It's like God won't let me talk. He wants me to really see the people who come week after week, hoping maybe this time something will change for them. Most are looking back at me with this sad expression. Their eyes are saying, 'Carlos, I'm trying so hard to do what you preach. And I can't. I don't know how to do it. Help me. Don't keep telling me more stuff to do. I haven't been able to do what you told me to do last week. I'm always failing. Please, help me, Carlos.' Right then it hit me—I didn't have nothing to give them. Just slick words, tough talk, and some fancy gestures. That morning I started to hate stepping into that pulpit."

Carlos is talking faster and faster. Most of the deck can hear him.

"Andy broke down all that madness," he says. "He'd say things like, 'So, Carlos, my preacher friend, what if you told them that God was crazy about them, that they didn't have to look over their shoulders? What if you told them that they didn't have to walk around carrying this big bag of religious 'ought-tos'? What if you told them that they weren't just saved sinners trying to appease a God who's way over there—" He gets up and runs across the deck. " 'What if you told them that they were saints?' " He strides back with his chin up. " 'That they were *saints* with a built-in ability to do great things? What if you taught them that if they believed, it would actually start to keep them from the wrong that's tearing them up? What if you told them that? Huh, big fella?' "

He's back in his chair now, peering right into my eyes.

"Andy's telling me this while I'm this big-time preacher at a church where every row is filled and everybody's stroking my ego and telling me how great I am."

"I thought your people were sad and discouraged," I say.

"Yeah, but I could still preach, man! Religious folk love getting the crap beat out of them by the preacher. It's like entertaining. And Carlos could flat-out work a room," he says, almost singing. He's up again. "My man, most of them are *looking* for guilt. Makes you look like you know what you're doing. And Carlos, my friend, Carlos always looked like he knew what he was doing."

He sits back down again as he says, "So I thought, *I can't preach what the old dude is saying. If I told my people those things, I'd be out of a job. They wouldn't need the magic dude of faith anymore.* That's what I thought. Sad. It was like I was living in two worlds—what Andy was telling me and what I was preaching. You know?"

I nod my head and look out at the buoys.

"No!" he suddenly blurts out. "Don't do that!"

I'm stunned. I don't know if this is part of his story or if he's talking to me.

"Don't do what?" I ask.

"Don't nod your head like you know, when you don't know. See, you *don't* know." His voice is rising. "Don't act like you know. It'll make you sick and fake and crazy... like I was."

His words hang in the air. The entire deck is suddenly quiet.

Carlos leans back in his chair and runs his hands through his thick black hair. He sighs deeply and draws in close.

"Oh, man, I'm sorry. Listen to me. Spouting to you all about grace, and I'm blowing up like some prison guard. Steven, I don't know you. I don't get to do that, man."

But I know he's right. I do this all the time—smile and nod knowingly. It's the worst form of insincerity. I insulate myself by pretending I get it.

"It's all right, Carlos," I say. "You were right. I was nodding and I didn't really know what you were talking about. It's a thing I do, like a reflex."

"No, man, that's not right. After you know me a while, maybe it's all right if I act like a maniac. But you're new here. You get to nod all you want. Forgive me, man?"

"It's all good, Carlos. Keep going. You were saying you were living in two worlds."

"Right. See, Andy was filling me with all this great truth. But it sounded too good to be true. It took me a while to be sure he wasn't hyping me. I tried it on real slow. Nothing scarier for Carlos than starting to let out what was true about me. Maybe that doesn't sound like much to a put-together suit with straight teeth. Oops. Sorry, I did the suit thing again, huh?"

I shrug. "That's all right. Thanks for trying."

"I mean, Jesus in Carlos Badillo on his worst freakin' day? The whole time I'm thinking, *You're kidding me! I'm a pastor, a religious dude. People don't want to know the real Carlos. People want to see a put-together Carlos. God may see me this way, but people don't want to. They want the bigger-than-life religious guy walking through the room, giving them a firm handshake, pat their kids on the head and make them feel important. That's what they want. Guys like me have taught them to see it that way. Right?"*

Instead of nodding, I say, "Right."

"I didn't have no giant failure deal going," he says, leaning in a little. "I wasn't sleeping with the choir or nothing, okay? I was just messed up like everyone else. But I thought you weren't supposed to let on. Like the moment we signed on—*poof*—you don't think about women wrong. You don't hate no one. You don't judge that dude down the street always showing off his shiny new boat out in the driveway. You don't resent people in your own church who can afford to hire people to mow their lawns. *Poof,* right? But you do, my man. You do! Everybody does. It's just they do it over different junk!"

Carlos sits back in his chair again. "So, when I finally believed that God really could handle Carlos without the pretend, oh, man, I couldn't run to it fast enough. It felt so good to not have to glue on the mask before I left the house. I couldn't go back. It was scary, and for a long time I almost wanted to go back. Just couldn't."

"What did the people in your church do?" I ask. "Didn't they judge you?"

"Yeah, some did. Big-time." He points and shakes his finger. "And they don't get a Christmas card from Carlos no more. But here's the deal: most who judged didn't really care about Carlos in the first place. Some people are always chasing ambulances, you know. Like they want to see others screw up so they can feel better about their own lives. How sad is that, man?"

"Yeah," I say. "Think I've done it myself a few times."

"Some did care, and they ran too. I've been tracking some of them down for a long time. But I caused that pain, man. I caused it by pretending, by hiding my failures from them. I regret the hurt I caused. A lot."

He picks up his glass of water. "But a lot of people stayed. And you know what happened? We got proven to each other. We all got to find out that God was really big—that He could handle all of us, the real us. It's like we looked around one day and said, 'So, you're still here, huh?' From that day on, I started to know what real was, what community was, what faith was, who God was."

He takes a big gulp of water. "Enough. You talk."

I blink a few times, trying to shake off his stream of words and get back to my own thoughts. "I don't know what to say. I don't know what I'm doing here. I guess I just thought it'd be nice for an old friend of my family to help me figure some stuff out. It—"

"You were lookin' for a good fixin'," Carlos says, interrupting. "Weren't you? A good fixin'."

He offers a knowing smile. "Ever notice that when someone tries to fix someone else, that person don't stay fixed? It's like trying to fix a Slinky by straightening it out and sitting on it. You ever own a Slinky, man? Sitting there, you think you've really got a handle on straightening stuff out. You're controlling your universe. You're all that. But no matter how long you sit, when you get up that Slinky springs right back. Only now it's all bent up too."

He suddenly pounds the table. "Steven, people don't ever get fixed. They either mature, or they just keep getting more bent up the rest of their lives."

I think of the other night up on the bluff. "Mature?" I ask.

"Yeah. Maturity is different. You can only mature and get real wisdom in community. Isolation produces the Unabomber."

I laugh out loud. And part of me realizes it's mostly the surprise that I'm actually enjoying hearing this stuff I'd usually avoid.

"Otherwise it's all information and arrogance, but no one gets wise and no one grows up. See, a guy like you, he's got skills. And skills can get honed in isolation. Then you show up like the hero with a shiny gizmo or something that makes everyone go 'Ooooooh!' Nobody can fire you 'cause you got skills. Folks maybe can't stand you, but they don't have a choice. So they just let you stay hidden. You don't have to go in for critique or nothing. And all the while you're walking around naked with a big old mole on your butt."

"What do you mean, they don't have a choice?"

"Well, you're the golden goose, right?" he says. "Because of what you can do, you start to think you're untouchable. And that's the problem, huh? You are untouchable. But there's a price tag: *your skill becomes more valuable than you.* What you bring is what's appreciated, not your presence."

I squint and he cringes. "Ouch. Huh, man? Happens all the time in bad marriages. What you bring home becomes more appreciated than the fact that you *are* home."

I stare at the table.

"I think I'm ticking off the golden goose, dude."

"No. You're fine."

"Andy once said to me, 'Carlos, what if there was a safe enough place where you could tell the worst about yourself and not be loved or respected less, but more?' You know what happens, Steven? Hidden junk we've been carrying around for years begins to melt away. People come alive. They start to discover who they really are. They start doing good stuff with their lives. They find their future. They stop needing to be right. They stop trying to fix their symptoms, and stop pushing everyone away.... They get loved."

Carlos chomps on another chunk of fish while speaking at the same time. "But trusting someone else with you? Come on. You gonna let someone start nosing around when you've been running the show for the last few decades? Ain't gonna happen. No way. Not until you get tired enough of shooting yourself in the foot."

*Is he describing me?*

He stops. "Hey, man, you gonna say something, or you just gonna grind those crackers into chalk?"

Before I can answer, Andy, Cynthia, and Hank are back at the table.

Hank pulls Carlos up out of his seat. "Let's go get me something to eat, Carlos."

"Something to eat? You've snatched food off every plate you've gotten near. Small countries would envy what you've had this afternoon."

Carlos looks at me. "Hey, well, I guess we're out of here. I gotta get him back to his probation officer."

Hank shrugs, resigned to his fate.

Carlos gives me a light whack on the back. "Great talking to you, man. Maybe you and me—we get to do this again, huh?"

"Yeah," I say, nodding. "I'd like that." Though I'm not certain I would.

Carlos and Hank slowly start to exit the deck. Carlos pats several people on the back while Hank uses the diversion to grab more table scraps. Everyone seems in on their routine.

"Well," Andy says, smiling. "Steven, you look as though you've had enough for today. Let's get you home."

Cynthia is back over at the next table closing her computer and gathering folders. "Another day, another half a phrase written. At this rate, I'll be publishing a trifold pamphlet." She looks over at me. "Dear, will we see you again? I really did enjoy meeting you, Steven."

Her bracelets are making that beautiful sound again, as if they were designed to be played against lacquered wooden restaurant tables.

"Steven, you're doing that thing where I'm speaking and you're not. Dear, promise me you'll work on the elements of conversation."

I smile at her. "I'll do better next time."

She smiles and reaches over to squeeze my hand.

I squeeze hers back. "Thank you, Cynthia. I really enjoyed meeting you."

With that, Andy winds me through brief introductions on the way out. As we step back into the Electra he asks, "So, how was your time with Carlos? He's a trip, huh? What did you two talk about?"

"Nothing much. Just talk."

*Why did I say that? He knows better. I know better. I do this all the time. I lie. No need to—I just do.*

*And why did I let Carlos lecture me? I don't do that.*

Andy and I are both quiet the rest of the ride to Fenton's.

I am surprised when he doesn't make any attempt to set up our next time.

"Thanks, Steven. I know it costs you a lot to give up an afternoon like that. I'm glad you got to meet Cynthia and the gang. Stay in touch."

As I step out of the Electra and back into my Mercedes it begins to rain. The streets are shiny and slick as I take an old and familiar route from Culver City into El Segundo. And I am alone again, heading back to Marriott room 643. The streets are whispering to me with the sounds of passing cars on wet asphalt. But it's as if I can't make out what's being said. I miss my wife. I miss my daughter. I want to be back in my home. But something is whispering to me. And I don't know what it is.

It's a whisper that's been there all my life.

# At a Table a Few Blocks from the Marriott

*(Saturday Morning, March 28)*

I'm sitting at a table in a restaurant a few blocks from the Marriott. Lindsey will be walking through the door in a few moments. She called Thursday evening to ask if we could get together this morning. We agreed to meet here. We haven't seen each other in seventeen days. I think this talk is probably about my coming home. None too soon. The housekeeping staff are leaving extra soaps, shampoos, chocolates, and shoeshine cloths, hoping for more tips. Much longer and I'll need to have a yard sale.

As she walks through the door I feel like a kid on a first date. We are both awkward. I get up to meet her.

"Hello, Steven," she says, offering a cautious hug.

"I ordered you some coffee," I say. "It should be here in a moment."

"Thanks. That's good."

"Good. I asked him to bring cream too."

Listen to us. We sound like foreign students in a class, learning conversational English. I almost expect one of us to ask where the library is.

We sit down and try to make small talk as we consider our menus.

Finally, Lindsey says, "I want this to work, Steven. I really do."

*What's that supposed to mean?*

"Yeah, so do I. I think I'm ready to make it work...I mean, better."

Our coffees arrive. She methodically stirs in the cream, tapping her spoon on the cup for a long time.

"Steven, I want you to know I love you. I've loved you almost since the day we met. That hasn't changed....I've really been trying to figure out what to do. I want to work this out together, not apart. But I also want to protect our family. I know what we're doing isn't a plan. I'm just buying time—"

I interrupt. "Lindsey, I think I can—"

"Please"—she motions with her spoon—"let me finish."

*Okay, this is not going as planned.*

"Steven, you need to be getting some help. It doesn't do any good to just have you staying in a hotel. That's not going to change anything. I don't know what you need, or who can help. I'm willing to get help with you, if that's what we need to do....I just can't take the thought of you coming home all nice and apologetic...until it all builds up again, to have you beat me down again. I don't think I could take that."

"Lin, I've kind of been meeting with someone."

"You have?"

"Yeah, sort of, I guess."

"Who is he?"

"Kind of a friend of the family."

"Is he a therapist? A counselor?"

"Not exactly." I realize trying to explain Andy might actually work against my case. Andy's probably not who she has in mind.

*This chain-smoking old marina guy started talking to me in a sketchy bar I never told you I went to and offered to drive me around. So we either sit up on a hill in his convertible or we go to this weird beach restaurant called Bo's. I really think he's the guy who can help me!*

*No, that's not gonna fly.*

I shrug my shoulders and mumble, "He's a friend of the family."

"Steven," she says, tapping her spoon again, "I really think I'm trying to say we just need some more time to figure this out."

*This is exactly what I was afraid of hearing.*

"How much more time were you thinking?"

"I don't know. I need to see something different. If you came home right now, it'd be better for a while. But what would change?"

"I really think it's different this time, Lindsey."

"That's what Alan said you'd say."

"Alan? Who's Alan?"

"Just a guy I met at the health club. He's a clinical counselor. He says that men say it's going to be different when they haven't dealt with anything but want life back to normal."

"That's the stupidest thing I've ever heard," I say, my voice starting to rise. I catch myself and try to regain a normal voice level. "Lindsey, so he's saying you can never say things are different, or you're faking it? Don't you see how stupid that sounds?"

It's quiet. Lindsey's tapping her spoon again, as if she's waiting for me to explode.

I look at her, wanting a response. "Well, don't you?"

She takes a last sip of coffee and says while getting up from her chair, "Steven, this isn't going right. We probably need to try this later."

"No, it's fine, Lin. Let's just talk."

"Steven, I'm still scared. I don't want to go anywhere. I want us back home together. This is not good for any of us. But it can't be like it was. Something really does have to be different. And I'm not hearing it today. I don't know what else to say. Let's talk on the phone about finding someone to help."

I decide anything I say is only going to make it worse. So I hug her and tell her I love her and let her go as I stay to pay for the coffees.

Ten minutes later I'm sitting in my car in the Marriott parking garage. And for the first time I realize this might not get better. She's never had the nerve to do this before. Now that she's risked it, she's not going to lose this chance. I have no idea what to give her to let her know it's going to be better. I feel like I'm losing my family. Jennifer probably has about given up on having a dad. I have no idea what she does when she goes to Molly's or most of the places she goes. When I ask her, she answers with as few syllables as possible. I don't know how to break into her life after spending so long outside. I feel as if we're one of those lights Andy talked about when we were up on the hill—a home where the daughter is pulling away though she never would have dreamed of it as a little girl.

And I know my wife. She wouldn't have brought up this guy Alan except to warn me about something that's probably already started to happen. My wife's letting herself fall for someone else.

I shuffle my way up to my room, past the lobby and the huge, clear container of fresh-mint-and-strawberry-infused water, past the smiling employees calling me sir, past the crowd of new guests excitedly drinking the mint water for the first time. Past the elevators with young families dressed for a day at the beach...to my room. I collapse on my bed, staring again at the picture of fruit. *I wonder if I could tip someone to get this crappy picture out of my line of sight.*

I grab the channel changer and find ESPN 2. It's early. My only option is nonconference college lacrosse—Akron against George Mason. It dawns on me that all the things I felt deprived of living at home, I can't drum up interest for now that I'm free to do them. What kind of irony is that? I am an important, sought-after, rising young executive, with enough money to do whatever I want, and I'm lying here on top of my shiny hotel bedcover in the middle of a Saturday watching nonconference college lacrosse.

George Mason wins 7–4.

# "Why Do You Enjoy Making Everything I Say Sound Stupid?"

*(Early Afternoon, Thursday, April 2)*

Day 22. Lindsey and I have not spoken since our meeting on Saturday. I worked in my room last night so I could justify taking part of the afternoon off today. I'm going to Bo's. Two months ago, I wouldn't have gone there on a bet. But for some reason, it seems like where I most need to be right now.

Bo himself greets me at the top of the patio steps. "Well, look what the catfish brung in. What the deal is with you? Better you look in da suit!" He yells out, "Hey everybody, the suit, he is back!"

I lean in toward the big man. "Bo, why are you doing that? Why are you calling me 'the suit'? I intentionally dressed down so you wouldn't call me that."

Bo just laughs, saying, "Suit is as suit does, *cher*." He slaps me on the back. "Git on in here now!"

Much of the crowd is the same. But there are some here today I don't recognize. And I don't see Carlos or Hank. But there, at the same table, are Cynthia and Andy.

Andy seems genuinely happy, surprised, and flustered to see me. "Steven! Hey, you came. Come here and join us."

He pulls out a clunky wooden chair and motions for me to sit.

"Welcome back. Did you give Bo your order? Never mind, he'll bring you what he wants anyway."

He stops a busboy and orders me an iced tea.

"You remember Cynthia."

Her flowing skirt is even more colorful than the one she wore last week. Bracelets dance across the table as she reaches for me. She stands and gives me a warm and genuine hug. I smile, feeling more welcome here than I do at the office I've been at for years.

"Hello, my dear," Cynthia says. "So, we didn't run you off completely, I see. It's so good to see you."

"Hello, Cynthia. How's the book coming?"

"Pamphlet, dear. A trifold pamphlet. And it's coming along fine."

These two are not what I'd expect out of mentors. She's sharp as can be, but neither of them seems very intentional about anything. They wouldn't last a month in my world.

A busboy distributes iced tea and a fresh glass of ice for Andy.

I look across the table. "So, let me try to piece things together here. Cynthia, whatever it is that Andy's been trying to do with me, you've been doing with him?"

"Something like that, I guess," she says.

"I've got a dozen questions. Andy here seems bent on answering every question *except* the ones I'm asking."

"Ask away, my dear," she says, adjusting her chair. "Ask away."

"Andy," I say, peering at him, "you okay with this?"

Andy nods. "It's actually one of the reasons I brought you here last week. Do you mind if I stay?"

"That's fine. So, Cynthia. Andy sets up a time to get together. He makes this big deal about us meeting. And I'm thinking we're really gonna get after some stuff. I don't know, whatever a counselor-type does. I've got some stuff to work on, and a wife who wants me to work on it, let's say. But Andy won't bite. It's like he doesn't take me seriously. To be honest, it feels like I'm wasting my time. Did you teach him that?"

She tilts her head as though she's not been asked this before. "Well, maybe a little bit of yes and no. I'd like to think I was probably a little more subtle than Andy can be." Cynthia gives Andy a knowing wink. "Let me see if this helps. Andy's really not so concerned right now about your particular issues."

"Is that so?" I smile sarcastically. "Well I, on the other hand, happen to be kinda concerned about my particular issues at the moment."

"Yes, I understand," she answers. "I mean, he's more listening for a way in, before he tries to approach those issues."

"Come on. That's so weak," I say. "That's what people in my world say when they don't know what they're doing."

"All right," she says. "Steven, do you mind if I treat you like a regular?"

*I know that language. It means, "I'm about to get in your face."*

"Whatever. I'd just like a straight answer from someone. You're all aware I have a job and a family, right? These little soirees aren't built into my schedule. I do have an actual high-pressure career here."

"Steven, your issues come and go, don't they, dear?" Cynthia asks. "Some will be with you for the rest of your life. But it's not like you solve a couple and then you're done. Two hundred and twenty some are waiting in the wings. Ones you can't even see or feel yet. You don't even know they're problems yet."

She's doing that too-close thing again, looking into my eyes as if she can't go on until she finds some kind of permission in there.

"Do you understand?" she asks. "Andy's looking for

access to the person named Steven. Nobody's had that for...well..."

"Maybe ever," I finish, giving Andy a glance. "It's not the first time it's been mentioned."

"Yes, nobody's had that for maybe ever," she repeats. "And all of this takes time. It's maddening if you're trying to fix this or that before anyone has access. Andy wants to stand *with* you in your issues. Because he knows nothing will change otherwise. So he's got to somehow—and here's the magic—create an environment where you'll feel safe enough. And I'm guessing that you, Steven, aren't nearly there yet, are you, dear?"

"Why do you say that?" I ask. "How do you know that? I'm here, aren't I?"

She puts her hand on mine. "Why don't you tell me? As much as Andy's gotten inside the wire on you a couple of times, hasn't this thought crossed your mind more than once? *This has been pretty nice. Maybe just getting away from my world a few times will help clear my head, give me some perspective. But it's probably the last time I'll get together with this guy. He's interesting and even has some insights that might actually help—if I weren't a rising executive but a marina operator.* Hmm?"

After a pause, looking away from Andy, I quietly answer, "Maybe a little."

She is silent again, still studying me.

"Yeah, *maybe*. See, Steven, you're the last person anyone should listen to about solutions for you because you've got it all distorted and you're convinced you're right. You live twenty-four hours a day in your self-contained world, where everything is about appearances, performance, bottom lines, leverage, and control. But the truth is, as confident as you try to appear, my guess is you don't feel adequate for the job. Don't get me wrong, you're pretty sure you're *all that*, but you're not sure everyone else agrees. So, you're worried, afraid that you're failing. You even blame yourself. But VPs aren't supposed to condemn themselves. "So you create this world where on one hand you hate yourself for what you suspect is true, and on the other hand you idealize yourself and blame others for not acknowledging the brilliance of this idealized person. Both of these make you blind to what God might be trying to tell you. And that's when the lights go out and you start tripping over end tables."

"Okay, hold on for a second," I say, shaking my head. "Cynthia, you're a lot of work, do you know that?"

"You're right, Steven. Look at me talking too much." She starts to get up, restacking pages she'd spread out at the table. "I should be writing. Instead, I'm meddling."

"No, it's not that. Please, sit back down." I wait until she does before saying, "It's just that I'm realizing it might not be best to drink when I'm with you all."

We all laugh.

"Steven, may I continue, then? This will only take a couple moments. I'm almost done with everything I know."

"Swing away," I say, sweeping my hand in her direction.

"Okay. So, my young friend, I would guess this has been your game plan so far. It's really quite funny when you step back and look at it. Maybe not so funny when it happens to be you. Anyway, try this on. You take a stab at figuring out your junk. But it doesn't bring any resolution. So you rehearse it, over and over. Still nothing. Then you find some allies you can explain your version of reality to. Maybe you get some temporary relief but still no resolution....See, Steven, this whole resolving-life-issues stuff is not like solving problems at work, is it?"

She waits for a response.

The answer is "No, it's not." She reaches over and pats my hand. "Stay with me here, dear."

We both laugh. How does she do that without making me feeling patronized?

"The solution," she continues, "isn't in getting more information. The solution isn't in getting others to see things your way or even in bringing more diligence to solve it. Now, are you ready, my dear? I'm about to say something harsh, but I don't mean it to be as rude as it will sound.

"The problem is you're a highly trained, intelligent, and successful professional, but when it comes to your personal life, you're a real amateur human being. Honey, you're as blind as a bat when it comes to you."

I laugh out loud. "You weren't kidding about the harsh-sounding part, were you? Cynthia, you blow me away. You're like this artsy lady about to show me pictures of her grandchildren. But I gotta tell you, my mother never says things like this to me."

"Honey, you should ask her," she says, laughing. "Maybe she'd like to!" She leans forward again. "Steven, do you want to know why you are clueless about you? Do you?" She stops again and stares. "Honey, I really need a verbal nod of some sort here."

"Yes," I say. "Yes, tell me why."

"It's because," she says slowly and dramatically, "you don't yet know who you really are. And Steven, you don't know who you are because you haven't yet learned grace."

I stop her before she can continue. "Oh, boy. See, there you go. That's all gibberish to me. I don't want to be mean, but you and Carlos, you sound like cult members. *Grace.* Do you have any idea what that sounds like? It's right up there with fluffy bunnies and unicorns. You're aware there's not a lot of grace talk in my board meetings. Look, I know you may not understand this, but in places where things get done, there's accountability, and quotas, and deadlines. You know what I think God wants? He wants all of us to take responsibility for what we're doing. Sorry, Cynthia. I was tracking with you. But if you wanna make sense to me, throw away the religious buzzwords."

Andy slaps his knee. "Whoo-eee! Yep, you got her there, Steven." He picks up his glass, swirling his ice. "Yep, first you start talking about grace. Next thing you know you're skipping Sunday school and sleeping in till noon. Then, a couple days later you're down at the dog track, drinking whiskey out of a paper bag and dating a showgirl named Tiffany!"

"Why do you enjoy making everything I say sound stupid?" I ask.

"I don't," he says. "I only enjoy making the stupid things you say sound stupid."

Cynthia takes over. "Steven, my friend, would you be offended if I told you that you sound to me like the one with the religious platitudes?"

"Meaning?"

"Meaning," she continues, "you sound like the one who's using religious concepts, and promoting them to others when they haven't even worked for yourself."

"Meaning?" I repeat.

"Meaning, grace is a gift only the nonreligious can accept. They're the only ones who can get it. They're the only ones who can use it. Religious folks see grace as *soft*. So they keep trying to manage their junk with their own willpower and tenacity. Nothing defines religion quite as well as a bunch of people trying to do impossible tasks with limited power while bluffing to themselves that it's working."

She leans even closer. "I just took in a lot of churches and religious institutions with that last statement."

"Did you hear that?" Andy laughs. "So, who's the religious one now, my friend?"

Cynthia smiles. "It takes a whole lot more than willpower

to get anything done in the human heart. You gotta allow yourself to receive something you can't find on your own."

Andy folds his arms and raises his eyebrows at me.

"You'll hear this next statement a lot around here, Steven," Cynthia says. " 'What if there was a place safe enough to tell the worst about you and still be loved just as much, if not more, for sharing it?' Do you know what happens?"

"Carlos says your stuff starts to get fixed."

"Resolved," Cynthia corrects. "And do you know what that safety is called? It's called an environment of grace. An environment where you can even say stuff as ridiculously naive and tired as the propaganda you've been holding on to."

I sit and stare at her a moment. Andy smiles and breaks the silence. "She's good, huh?"

"I'm not sure at this particular moment," I say, even though I have little doubt.

"So, to answer your question from before," she says, "someone has to break that pattern if anything's going to change. That's why Andy won't bite at trying to fix what you're throwing at him. Now, lots of people don't like this answer, and they go back to trying to fix their lives with mediocre ability. You can fool yourself quite a while, playing that game. But if you're tired of the cycle and actually consider some of this, you might just get healthy."

"Okay, enough, both of you," I call out. "My head hurts."

"Good," Andy replies. "Our work here is done."

"One more question," I say. "Then I do have to go. We all know I have an issue with anger. I also know you don't think it's my most critical one. Andy, you said that Cynthia helped you work through some stuff that you'd ignored for a long time. What stuff was that?"

He taps his watch. "Gee, you're gonna miss that meeting."

"I'll be fine. Are you gonna answer my question?"

Cynthia interrupts. "May I answer it?"

"Sure," I say, taking a drink of my tea. "Right now I'm just looking for some dirt on Andy to get the attention off of me."

Cynthia doesn't laugh at my joke. "You may not like what you're going to hear. I don't like telling it."

She motions to the busboy. "Dear, would you be so kind as to refresh this young man's drink? Thank you."

She looks at Andy and then out to the ocean. She is much less animated, much less immediate.

"At the time of Laura's death, Andy was running an incredibly successful Forbes-rated company in Newport Beach. He was the golden boy of the South Coast financial world."

"I oversaw an incredibly talented team of commodity portfolio analysts," Andy says.

"Yeah. I actually figured that out a while ago."

"That so?" Andy throws me a sideways glance. "Over time I got Langston Group into a pretty strong position. Top two or three in the western states."

"Big name. I first heard about Langston in my teens."

"For the first five years there," Cynthia says, taking over, "everything Andy touched was golden. But there was something sinister working in the background from back to his childhood. Laura could see it but married him anyway. That woman loved him so. But he carried this deep sense of inadequacy that was driving him to not fail at all costs."

"That's called shame," Andy says.

"Over the years he carried it to high school sports and then to college and the girls he dated. And now here he was, finally in a place where preparation, hard work, and skill met opportunity. He worked like a dog, trading family and sanity for turning that company into something that would..."

Andy helps her. "Prove something to someone."

"Oh, dear." Cynthia is now looking directly at me. "This wasn't a case of misplaced priorities. For Andy, every victory, each procurement was more proof, more vindication of his worth. But his drive was beginning to undermine his empire. Others could see it and tried to help. But all he could see were forces standing against the proof of his value as a leader. He hated who he was becoming, but he refused to lose. He began justifying more high-risk deals."

Both Cynthia and Andy are silent for a moment.

"Then Laura got sick," Andy says. "She needed me more than ever. I was too focused on keeping the rocket soaring. It tore me up and hurt her incredibly. I—"

He stops. His eyes are full of tears.

"I began justifying more and more questionable practices, more risky ventures. Word got out to deep-pocket investors that the Langston Group was no longer a safe bet. I panicked. Two months before Laura's death, I started to turn a blind eye to some of what I had put in motion. Then Laura died and I kept working. But I couldn't think as clearly. I lost any sort of subtlety and began exposing accounts to enormous risk."

"Wow," I say. "I'd never think you could have done that."

"And then she was gone," he says. "Just gone. The only person who'd ever made sense of me was gone. I was completely out of control. One day I'd be unable to get out of bed, the next I'd be making million-dollar decisions with my eyes closed. Five months after Laura's death, it all came tumbling out. The whole thing. I was fired. I would never work in finance again."

"I'm sorry, Andy."

"Thanks," he says. "I needed you to hear this."

All three of us are silent.

Andy finally starts again. "Steven, if you'd asked me what

was wrong in the months before I was exposed, I would've said, 'I need to get some rest, go on a vacation. I'm tired and Laura's illness has been a real strain on our marriage.' I might have mentioned some behaviors—working too hard, impatience, getting easily frustrated—but they were all symptoms. I couldn't and wouldn't allow myself to risk seeing what had been sabotaging me all my life."

Cynthia's hand is now on Andy's arm. "That answer could come only by someone offering him a safe place, someone who could handle the worst about him. Only then did Andy stop pretending. Only then could he begin to look at the worst of who he was without being destroyed by it."

"I think that may be enough for today," Andy mumbles.

"Wait, what about—"

Andy looks really uncomfortable all of a sudden. "Right now, if you don't mind, I think I just need to go home."

Cynthia and Andy stand up to hug each other. They embrace for a long time. No words are spoken. Andy reaches for my hand, gives me a weak smile, and walks away.

I clumsily say good-bye to Cynthia and excuse myself.

Driving back to work, I decide to call Andy. He picks up after a couple of rings.

"So I feel stupid pressing you," I say. "I don't know if you've noticed, but sensitivity is not my strong suit."

"Steven." Andy's voice is calm, more subdued than normal. "I've come to believe that there are no *together* people. Only those who dress better than others."

We both offer weak laughs the way people do when they're trying to cover an awkward moment.

Andy continues. "It's a myth about needing superior religious folks to impart truth to the rest of us. Such people do not exist. Only those who think they are. Each of us, Steven, walks with a profound limp. Some have just learned to hide their limps better. Don't ever trust anyone who makes you feel intimidated by their presence because of some aura of religious superiority. People like that are almost always hiding something—incredible arrogance or a secret depravity that would shock you."

I say nothing, listening carefully as I drive, not wanting to stop his reflections.

"I don't want any pretend superiority. I can't hide well enough to pull that off, even if you want me to. I don't want to intimidate you. I want to be someone who's vulnerable and authentic. That's the only ace I carry up my sleeve. I'm learning the power of love to heal me. I am trusting Him *with* me. No other cards, no other sleeves. No other nothing."

For a moment it's quiet on the other end of the line. Then he says, "Thank you for giving me the privilege of today, my friend. Don't go away, okay?"

Suddenly I feel embarrassed for him and want to get out of this phone call.

"Hey, I've got another call coming in," I say. "It's the office. I'd better take it. I'll see you later, Andy." I quickly hang up.

There was no other call. I'm a liar. A liar who will avoid vulnerability at any cost.

Later that evening, I'm brushing my teeth in front of that lit pull-out circular mirror that makes your nose hairs look really big. I'm just staring... at me. But tonight it's different. It's like I'm trying to see who's in there. *More stuff I never do.* But suddenly, right here, tonight, I can't turn away.

*What do people see when they look at this face? Is Carlos right? A guy they have to endure but don't want to be around?*

My harangue is interrupted by a ding from the other room signaling the arrival of a new e-mail. It's Andy.

Steven,

I'm free tomorrow morning. My Fridays are usually pretty busy, but I'd like to come by your office if you wouldn't mind. I don't need a lot of time. You could drop in and out as necessary. I'd just like to see more of your world. Shoot me an address and tell me where I can sit, like a fly on the wall. I won't embarrass you by smoking in the lobby or wearing my Hawaiian shirt with the hula girls on it. I still have some respectable clothes I can dig up.

See you Wednesday.

Andy

*No. I don't want him at my work.*

Minutes later I'm lying in bed trying to figure out why. Maybe it's because who I am at work and who I want Andy to see are two really different people. I turn off CNN and spend the next hour staring at the darkness, defending myself and devaluing Andy and his friends. But my pitiful charade disgusts even me. I'm like a sixth grader hiding magazines from his mom. I slowly shake my head in the dark. The next morning I e-mail Andy.

Andy,

I've got some time between 10:45 and 11:30. I've attached a map. Have the receptionist call me, and I'll meet you in the lobby.

Please don't wear a suit. I don't think I could handle it.

S.

# "God, What Are You Doing to Me Here?"

*(Friday Morning, April 3)*

I'm staring at my screen, waiting for the call that Andy is in the lobby.

*What is my problem? I've got a top-floor office overlooking one of the most expensive and vital business districts in the country. I'm VP of one of the most innovative and successful companies in Southern California. He's a marina operator. Chill.*

I glance at my watch for the eleventh time in as many minutes. It's 10:42.

*God, what are You doing to me here? Why did You let this guy into my life?* I lean back in my chair and stare at the ceiling.

*I want to shut down this whole thing with him. But I have this sense that if I don't face this stuff, whatever it is, it's going to ruin me. And... if I do face this stuff, it's going to ruin me.... Maybe I should just get sick. I feel like I'm coming down with something. Yeah, maybe I need to go home, cancel this meeting.*

I'm snapped out of my daze by the receptionist's voice. "There's an Andy Monroe here to see you."

As I turn the corner into the lobby, my fears are realized. Andy's talking to board vice chairman Phillip Castleman and human resources director Whitney Rhodes. *Great. They've seen more of my worst than anyone but my wife.*

Phillip sees me crossing the courtyard and yells out,

"Steven, you didn't tell me you were friends with Andy Monroe. I've know this old carpetbagger for decades. We go back to the MBA program at Pepperdine."

"Well, hey, how about that?" I respond with a weak smile.

*This is not unlike former girlfriends at a sleepover, comparing notes. I'll bet Castleman has been feeding Andy all sorts of dirt about my status around here.*

"Hey, look, I hate to break this up," I say, "but Andy came to see *me*, thank you."

As Whitney walks away, she counters, "Fine, but Andy and I are having lunch together. And no, you can't join us."

Phillip says to Andy, "I'll see you around noon, when you and Steven are done. Deal?"

"Deal," Andy calls back, as Phillip disappears into the crowd intersecting the lobby.

Andy and I grab a couple of lattes from the second-floor coffee shop and sit down in front of a secluded picture window overlooking the enormous lawns and ponds sprawling in front of the complex. Andy seems quite taken with it all, rising from his chair and standing and staring. I'm talking a mile a minute about nothing. Certain I've just been the topic of conversation, I just can't face what he's going to say when I stop.

"This is absolutely beautiful, Steven," he finally says, interrupting my babble. "What an incredible view."

I jerk back to the present. "Yes, it is. I hide up here. Nobody much comes to this spot. Sometimes this is the only place in the whole complex where I can make sense of anything."

"You're kidding me. Nobody? See, I'd think people would be staring out this window all day long. I would—I may, actually! I might apply for a job in the coffee shop just so I can come up on break and look out this window."

Then it's quiet, as we both know something needs to be said, but neither of us appears to know how to approach it. The suspense is killing me, so I begin. "Look, I think I know what you and Phil were talking about."

"Steven..."

"Please, I need to get this out. Let me give you my version." I dive in. "First, I'm sure he mentioned there's talk about canning me. That's a half-truth at best. Yeah, there are some on the board who want to get rid of me, but honestly, from where I sit, it's jealousy. I'm thirty-four. Most of them are in their late forties. You do the math."

"Steven, it's not like that."

"Andy, it's okay. I like Phil. He's a good guy. He's gone to bat for me on several occasions. But for all appearances, his hands aren't clean. He's got his own butt to cover. Finding a younger scapegoat is a convenient way. I'm not saying I've done everything perfectly. But until they give me some room to create my team, I'm set up for failure. I'm covering for half the positions in this place. I can do in half the time what most of these six-figure kiss-ups are doing in their safe jobs. For all the talk of innovation it's no more than a good-old boys club.

"And I can't believe Whitney wants to talk with you!"

"I asked to have lunch with *her.*"

I pause. "You did? Listen, I'm sorry. I just think maybe you need to hear both sides before you make assessments."

He's silent, staring out the window. And I start to wonder if I may have misread the situation.

Andy stares out the window for a long time. "Are those mallards, Steven? Am I looking at mallards? You've got mallards in that pond, don't you? Never can really tell what makes one a duck, the other a mallard. I guess they're both ducks. But those are mallards, aren't they?"

I can't believe this guy. "Did you hear a thing I said?"

"Oh, yeah, sure. Every word." He nods while still gazing out the window. "It's just that you've got a veritable marshland out your window here. I've never seen anything like it! I'm expecting hippos or gators to emerge from those reeds at any moment. I need to come fishing here. You think they'd mind? Oops, sorry. Forget I asked. You're the 'they,' aren't you?"

"Were you listening to me, Andy?"

"Yep."

"Then what did I say?"

"Well, I think you were telling me your version of reality so I could make a better assessment of what to believe."

"And?"

He turns and slowly walks to a seat directly across from me. He thumps the bottom of his coffee cup with his index finger. "Well, Steven, the trouble is, now I've only got one version."

"What do you mean?"

"I mean, nobody told me anything."

"What?" I shake my head in disbelief. "Phil didn't talk to you? You and he and Whitney weren't..."

"Nope. Just talk. 'Is-your-brother-still-with-Intel?' kind of stuff. There *was* some lively discussion about the clam chowder here, which led to a lunch invitation."

It's quiet again. I'm staring out at the pond, watching a pair of geese glide peacefully across its surface. Across the room there is a clatter of silverware. Someone is asking the girl behind the register for a packet of Splenda.

"I don't know what to say," I mumble.

"What do you *want* to say?"

"I don't know. I want out of this moment."

"So, go ahead. Maybe you have a call on another line?"

I look over at him. He's wearing a smile that says, *Gotcha.*

"There was no other call the other day."

"I was in business once too, remember?"

"Andy, I'm the head of marketing in the very company I dreamed about when I came out of the University of Washington. Nearly every indicator would say I'm doing a really good job. The *Wall Street Journal* did an article on me two months ago. *Me.* I've arrived. And now something I can't seem to control or even name is about to sabotage me. And none of my training has prepared me to solve this one."

Andy looks into my eyes. "Well said, my young friend."

I get up and take my place at the window.

"Last evening I was in a restaurant with half a dozen colleagues after a leadership meeting. Somewhere between drinks and dinner, I found myself sitting back, observing conversations from the outside. Half listening, half staring, I kept drifting back to lunch with your friends at Bo's. I was hit by a couple things."

I glance back to Andy. He's grinning.

I look back out the window and say, "Sometimes I wish I'd never met you. Do you know that?"

"Yeah, my wife said the same thing a time or two." He chuckles. "So you were about to give me some observations."

"No one in this company knows me," I say. "I've been with these people, most of them, for over two years. We talk sports, the economy, rival companies, product; we gossip about those who don't show up; we tear others down; we make dry and sarcastic humor. It's fast and clever and hip. Most of the time I'm in the middle of it. But I can't come up with one time when anyone asked me how I was really doing.

"I've been dying inside these last few months, and no one sees it or wants to see it. For all I know, everyone around me is melting down too. But I'd never ask. We all act shocked when someone leaves or implodes from the pressure. But really, everyone anticipates it. It's part of the package that comes with the long hours, the privilege, and the privacy of what we do. Andy, I'm thirty-four, and I'm learning more every year how to keep people from really knowing me. These last few months I'm finding I really hate it."

Andy nods. I can tell he's really listening. "You said you had a couple observations?"

"Yes," I continue. "I'm a Christian. Actually, I've been a Christian at most about nine hours a week. At church—when we go. I was a Christian praying with my daughter on the rare nights I was home before she went to bed. And I'm a Christian on the board of an inner-city ministry in Inglewood. All I do is show up and offer to pray, really, but the rest of the time I don't really have a role. My relationships are purely utilitarian. I have the camaraderie here that profiting from defeating financial enemies brings. But it's nothing like Bo's. If any of us dared show weakness, we'd be torn apart. There's no real affirmation or friendship, just the boasting in a job well done. You don't trust and you aren't trusted. We're just well-paid mercenaries."

"So why are you telling me this?"

I look down at my coffee. "You were in business once too, remember?"

"Fair enough. Do you want to continue?" he asks.

"I think I do." I take a deep breath. "Anyway"—I motion with my hands at the buildings around us—"I carry this world home. I think I love Lindsey, but mostly I try to buy her off, appease her. I fake interest in the events of her day by nodding and giving the appropriate responses. But much of the time I'm somewhere else, rehearsing all the undone garbage in front of me. I do it almost without noticing."

Andy stands up and slaps his hands together. "Well,

look, it's the middle of a pretty busy workday. I've already taken up too much of your time. Steven, I know this is thin consolation, but I'm really proud of you. I think you'll look back on these few minutes and say that this may be where things started to turn."

I turn from the window. "You know, just when I think I'm starting to figure you out, you say something like that."

Andy laughs. "I just wanted to say it so that when it happens you'll think, *Hey, that marina guy was pretty sharp after all.*" He places a hand on my shoulder. "So, listen, I'm gonna go meet with Phil and then have an innocent lunch with Whitney, and then I'm out of your hair. We won't talk about you. I promise. I've just got to get to the bottom of this whole chowder issue, or it'll eat at me all afternoon."

I shake my head. "Andy, you're a very odd man."

"I'll take that as a compliment," he says, pretending to tip his hat.

"Before you go, I want to ask you something about Bo's. I don't know, I think... it did something to me." I look down at my shoes. He stands back and folds his arms. I feel weird telling him this. "It's like I got a picture of what things could be like. There's something there I don't get. But I want to. Do you think I could drop by again sometime?"

"Hey, I don't get to pick the crowd," he says. And just like that, Andy gets up to leave. "Steven, thanks for this. Did Phil ever tell you he once climbed out of one of those little suspended cars in the Peter Pan ride at Disneyland? He was dangling from the side and trying to use his feet to knock over one of the steeples in the little pretend town below. Disney guards kicked him right out of the park. Gave him a lifetime ban. True story. I mean, who do *you* know who's been banned for life from Disneyland? Charles Manson never got a lifetime ban."

Walking away he yells back, "Hey, thanks for taking the risk of letting me hang around here." He smiles and then whistles his way down the stairs, two steps at a time.

I work late before heading south. I think I'm avoiding going back to my room. I think the staff is beginning to feel sorry for me. I've been there longer than some of them. They don't even bother putting that sign on the sink about my towels anymore. I guess they figure I've made up my mind about wasting their water.

The lobby is mostly empty as I walk through to the elevator. My shoes are making that conspicuous *click-clack* echo across the marble floor. There's a new kid behind the counter. He can't be eighteen. As I walk by he beams brightly and says, "Hello, sir. Welcome to the Marriott." I feel like saying, "Kid, I *am* Mr. Marriott. You're fired." But I'm too tired.

Back in my room, I peel an orange and set up my laptop before changing out of my work clothes. I see another e-mail from Andy. It's titled "I don't care what you say, I'm fishing in that lake!"

I open it and scroll down.

Steven,

Okay, so we've been at this for about three weeks. It's time for an exam. This exam is not about you. It's about me. I'm figuring you're asking if this old guy is someone you can trust.

So, let's grill me and see if I can take it. Why do I want to help you?

Because I learned that until I finally trusted someone enough to open up to them, I could never find what I was after, and I want the same for you.

I don't want your trust for my benefit, but for yours. I will never demand it. At the end of the day,

I can't ask you to drum up something that isn't there. I can only ask your permission to earn it. Trust is a right response to another's love. For some it is the most natural response in the world. But some of us have learned, over time, through hurt or all sorts of junk, to not receive it from anyone. And so sometimes a friend needs to ask another friend to let him in. You see, I think you got seriously hurt somewhere along the line and closed yourself off to people. I also think something very important happened today. I could be wrong, but I'm pretty sure you started tipping some of the cards in your hand. You pulled 'em right back, but I swear I saw a couple. You're not used to doing that; nobody sees your cards. Maybe you're regretting that now, hoping to pull the cards even closer. I expect that.

But everything's gonna get tested from here on out. See, the old guy knows too much now! Who I am really starts to matter now, doesn't it? Sometime, maybe next time, I won't just listen; maybe I'll respond. I might just challenge you at some deeply personal place. You may fear that, but something in you hopes for it too.

Steven, I will never ask that you agree with me. But we'll be wasting each other's time unless at some point you *give me permission.* You don't have to, but I'm guessing you'll bump around and hit your shins a lot more if you don't. Either way, it's a crapshoot. But, hey, I'm mixing my gambling metaphors, aren't I?

I can hear you saying, *I thought I already gave you permission. I'm carving out time from my life for this crap. If I'm not letting you, then what have I been doing?*

You've been testing me to see if I'm for real. It may

have looked like I was testing *you,* but I don't need to test you to see if I can trust. I've already decided. I'm in.

So if you're still reading at this point, I'd like you to ask yourself if I fit these descriptions. These are characteristics of what you might call a "healthy protector." First, do I see others as sinners trying to be saints, or as saints who still sometimes fail? Is it my goal that something will get conquered or fixed, or that nothing will remain hidden? That one's huge. Read that again. There are very few places where the value of no hiding is placed above getting the other person "better." Oh, and this is huge too: do I care more about getting your issues resolved or establishing a healthy relationship so the issues can be resolved?

There probably have been some people and will be many more in your life who offer direction and insight. But if those attributes aren't there, in spades, you've got the wrong guy. He can give you some techniques to control your behavior. That and $3.50 will get you a fancy coffee drink. But he won't be able to stand with you in solving your issues. He'll have tools for inspiration and, at best, a lot of sincerity; and guilt, shame, and performance standards at worst. He'll always make sure you know he's the teacher, the one in charge. But he'll never risk standing with you in your struggles and truly sharing himself with you. Because at the end of the day it's all about that person being something for God. It's a notch on his religious belt. He takes little risk, and pays no cost. It's just more technique, more practiced advice, more slogans, and his hands stay clean. He may stoop down to help a dullard now and then, but he's not in it for anyone but himself. You're gonna want to stay clear of that guy.

I'm figuring I may look like that guy to you at times. I'm not. What *I* get out of this is not what I'm after.

Steven, you spoke about the difficulty of meshing your work world with your spiritual life. You said that no one would dare show weakness or he'd be torn apart. I get that. I have known that world. Most men and women do.

It reminds me of a statement one of Steinbeck's characters, Doc, makes in *Cannery Row*:

> It has always seemed strange to me . . . The things we admire in men, kindness and generosity, openness, honesty, understanding and feeling are the concomitants of failure in our system. And those traits we detest, sharpness, greed, acquisitiveness, meanness, egotism and self-interest are the traits of success. And while men admire the quality of the first they love the produce of the second.

It took failure for me to realize that there's a profound "produce" created when the best in people is coupled with humility. It lacks none of the accomplishment and gains an integrity that allows everyone to enjoy what the product brings. I think your future is in that quote.

So, who am I? That's the question Steven Kerner should be asking right now. Well, you know some. You know a little of my failures. But you need to know more. My life is still messy. I'll disappoint you, and

I'm sure I'll exasperate you again, whether it's my inconsistencies, petty selfishness, or something else. I may even hurt you by being stupid and insensitive. I don't want to, but I probably will. Still, I won't hide from you. Sometime, after you get to know me better, you may *wish* I'd hide. . . .

You see, nobody *ever* arrives. I certainly haven't. We just learn to depend and trust better. Eventually we can grow more mature and become better friends to others. We can learn how to love while learning to be loved. And we can learn how to offer protection in exchange for permission.

Well, enough. I leave you with this: How many country-western singers does it take to screw in a lightbulb? Three. One to screw in the new lightbulb and two to sing about losing the old one.

I've got a million of 'em. Seriously, somebody stop me.

In the grace of Jesus,

Andy

## "We Should Talk."

*(Saturday Morning, April 4)*

I decide to write Lindsey. We talk on the phone every day. But I want to say something important so I decide to put it in writing. Recently, when we talk about anything beyond bills, appointments, and picking up Jennifer, it gets all garbled and I sound like I'm selling soap. So I send an e-mail:

> Lindsey,
>
> Last Saturday morning about this time we were making really clumsy conversation over coffee. You told me I needed to be meeting with someone. I told you I was, but didn't explain much. Well, I've had quite a ride this last month. The night we got into the fight I came home late. You need to know where I was. I haven't been doing well. Like for a long time. I don't talk much about it, because I don't usually know what to say. So, a bunch of times, I'd leave work early and just drive around escaping into some music or something. Usually I'd end up at this place called Fenton's. It's a dumpy little dive in Culver City where my family used to go when I was growing up. Anyway, that afternoon I'm sitting in the parking lot like half a dozen other times. But this time I go in. And I meet this old friend of my dad's, only I don't know who he is.

Remind me to tell you about that some time; like when you've had a couple margaritas. Anyway, his name is Andy. We've driven around in his car a few times. He says I've been deceiving myself, that I can't see myself clearly and I need to trust others to help me. I think he's a Christian, but not like most I know. So, I agreed to go for lunch at this place called Bo's Café. There's this interesting group of people who meet there on Thursdays. It's been going on for a few years. The place is right where I used to hang out down at the beach as a kid. So now I go there sometimes. I'm not sure why. They're all great people, but it's more than that. It's like some of them can see me for who I am and really listen, like they like me. I know that sounds stupid, but I don't have many people I can say that about right now. And I've never been anyplace like it. I have no idea what I'm learning. But I wanted you to know something is happening. So . . . there. That's all I wanted to say. I love you and Jennifer. Tell her I'll see her on Wednesday after school, at 3:30.

Love,
Steven

Lindsey responds:

Steven, I wanted you to know that your words are very important to me. I'm proud of you and what you're doing. Andy sounds great. So does Bo's.

I know you don't have to do this. You could be trying to force things right now. I appreciate you explaining this to me, and giving things time. It sounds like Bo's is exactly what you need right now. Maybe good things will come out of it. We should talk soon about when it might make sense for you to come home. Thanks again for your note. Jennifer says she'll meet you at the circle in front of her school.

Love,
Lindsey

# Out of Excuses

*(Late Morning, Tuesday, April 14)*

I work about three miles from Bo's. I grew up less than seven miles from the pier where the restaurant now stands. Many summer days, a bunch of us would ride bikes down there from Culver City. I would have been twelve or so, a little over twenty years ago. We'd fish from the pier with line and weights we'd pocketed from Ronnie Oliveri's older brother's tackle box. We'd use sardines right out of a can as bait and catch some pretty freaky-looking stuff. Creatures that would sting your hands, ink your clothes, and smell up your backpack. Back then we didn't know there was a Marina del Rey or Venice Beach. There was just this exciting, dangerous world that belonged all to us. I still can't believe our parents let us come down here.

Parts of the neighborhood were sketchy even then. Not far from where Bo's is was this Italian place. I just remember the checkered-tile floor was always greasy. They sold immense triangles of pizza. Huge, oily pieces of heaven. One day Wally Miller actually ate six pieces—pepperoni, sausage, and all. Nobody ever came close to that record. Later, he threw it all up on the boardwalk, but that just added to the legend.

Most of us swam in cutoff jeans. The ride home at the end of the day seemed like a three-day odyssey. There is no rash quite like that made by sand, wet underwear, and a one-gear bicycle.

Then came girlfriends, sports, and cars. Most of us no

longer went down to that stretch of beach anymore. It was too much a part of childhood. We were grown up now. We'd take our girlfriends to Hermosa or Manhattan, even up to Santa Monica, but rarely down to the seedy Venice Beach of our youth. Then college took me to Washington and a couple of marketing jobs. When I came back to Southern California, it was for this position at Visratech. I never even visited my old home in Culver City, never went back to any of my old haunts.

It's been almost two weeks since I've been at Bo's. During that time I've taken a couple more rides with Andy in the Electra. But the newness is gone. I'm starting to think this whole thing isn't really going anywhere. Maybe it was only "Detroit magic" after all. This whole season has been one of those out-of-the-ordinary things you do once or twice in your life, and when you look back, you realize they kind of turned things around. But now it looks like things are getting back in perspective. I think I may be just about done with Bo's and these rides. I'm pretty sure I'll be home very soon. I just had to get outside the issues for a bit. Bo's has been good for that.

And Andy . . . I think he's a really nice guy with some good insights who just likes to talk. Honestly, I think he's getting as much from me as I am from him. I'm like the son he's never had. I also think it's probably pretty important to him that a younger, successful businessman finds his wisdom helpful. That's fine, but there's a limit to how deep I want to go with all of this. Whatever their deal is with permission and protection, it's all too slow and soft for my pace. Maybe I'll keep coming to Bo's from time to time. Why not? They're a pretty great group of people. Most of them can't even understand my life; they don't have to. But I'm sure not going to turn over my dirty laundry to people who couldn't hold a position two levels beneath me at Visratech.

But I'm back at Bo's today. I'm dropping in unannounced. I'm immediately greeted by Bo's booming voice. "Where's the suit?"

"Hey, Bo," I say, reaching out my hand. "Well, the suit kind of seems a little out of place around here."

"Oh, yeah, it does, *cher*." He laughs. "You come in lookin' like a symphony conductor, and we got us a deckful of banjo players." He laughs until he starts hacking like a man with tuberculosis.

"Hey then," he rasps, catching his breath, "how you likin' that shrimp cocktail last time?"

"It was great, Bo."

"Well, get it out of yo' head," he says, glaring suddenly and leaning in at me. "We got no shrimps today. We got us five-day-old snapper with worms. That's what you're gettin' and yo' gonna like it."

I know the routine now. "Okay, then, snapper and worms it is."

"Good. You lookin' for Andy? He's not here yet. What the deal is with that boy?"

I shrug. "Don't know. Didn't call him. I just thought I'd stop by. Take my chances, see who's here."

"You got Hank and Carlos. So snapper and worms gonna look like an improvement." He laughs again then yells out to the kitchen as he walks away, "One snapper with worms for the deck crowd!"

I'm greeted warmly by the group, already a couple dozen strong. Carlos pulls out a chair for me.

"Hey, Steven. Great to see you, man. What's up?" He looks me over, sizing up my clothing selection.

"You're looking fine, my man. Nice uniform. Most of you important dudes dress like this when you're trying to act all casual. You got your starched khaki slacks and your pastel shirt with the little crocodile guy on it. I love that little guy. He's cool. Nothing says, 'I'm a relaxed, important dude,' like that crocodile shirt tucked into a pair of starched pants. Nice."

He laughs and reaches for my hand. "Hey, I'm just playing with you, man. It's good to see you, Steven."

I reach back and give his hand a firm shake. "So, where's Andy?"

"He was here a little bit ago," Hank answers, "but he had to get back down to the marina. So what are you ordering?"

I tilt my head. "I think snapper with worms."

Others on the deck continue to greet me. Only after everyone settles back into their routines does Carlos lean in to ask, "So, how's it been going?"

"What do you mean? With what?" I look back and forth between the two.

"You know," Carlos says, "the rides with Captain Andy?"

I tip my head back a little. "Oh. Well, that's a good question. I was just thinking about that on the way over." *I'm not sure how much to say.*

Hank grins. "You're not sure how much to say, are you? I mean, you barely know us, and we're asking to see your dirty underwear."

"Once again, my friend"—Carlos groans, pushing his bread bowl of chowder away—"you have proven your knack for ruining my lunch."

"You flatter me," Hank says, eyeing the remains of the bread bowl. "You mind?"

These two are like an old married couple on a cruise. "Hank, you're right," I say. "I *don't* know how much to tell you."

Hank forks a piece of the huge shrimp cocktail just placed

in front of me. "You don't have to tell us anything. You just have to be willing to share your food."

"Fair enough."

"Want to know his game plan?" Carlos asks abruptly.

"What do you mean?"

"I've been watching the old man for over three years now," Carlos says, leaning back, putting his hands behind his head. "He's one of those rare cats who learned something profound about halfway through life. Most never get it. His failure gave him a great gift. Got him off track long enough to start listening and seeing. He got to see life for real, after there's not so much to lose. Changed his whole way of seeing the world, his friendships, his lifestyle. Took a lot of his fears away. Made him a lot more fun to be around."

"So what did he learn?" I ask.

Hank beams. "This is so cool!" he says. " 'What did he learn?' Like Frodo asking questions about Gandalf! I love this stuff!"

Carlos shakes his head and continues, "Andy figured this out—there's a stinking huge difference between influence and the authority you get with a title."

"Any dolt can stumble into a title," Hank barks. "Lots of people with big-sounding titles have people under them listening only because they have to."

Carlos nods. "Yeah. Almost anyone can teach information. I've only met a handful who are allowed to really influence."

I'm listening, but with Andy not here, I decide to change the subject.

"So, tell the truth. Do you guys ever feel like it's not going anywhere?" I ask. "Like nothing ever gets solved? I mean, 'Come on,' I want to say, 'let's just get on with it.' What does the guy need from me, a note from my parents? You guys know what I mean, right?"

The two of them look at each other, like they're trying to figure out who should answer. Carlos wipes his hands and face on his napkin as he responds.

"Look, Steven. I like you, man. A lot. But I gotta tell you, here's how it goes. A big guy like you, maybe you're willing to invest a couple more times for a payoff. That's how it goes down in corporateland, huh? This time or next, Andy's gonna give you a magic one-liner or two that'll set you free. You're used to shiny packaging, man. Unless the container looks like what you expect, you get all patronizing and condescending. You understand condescending?"

I glare at him. "Yes, I understand condescending."

"So you'll get impatient when Andy doesn't give you the shiny, clean package, and pretty soon we won't see you no more. Look, Steven, this whole deal is not about some little behavioral technique—fix a bad habit or learn new skills to mask your behaviors. Because little techniques, they don't do squat. They just fail you, man. Next time you'll be even more cynical and all closed off. Soon you'll stop letting God get your attention in a parking lot, huh? You just settle in and figure this is as good as it gets. So the rich dude buys enough toys and keeps busy enough to pretend it doesn't hurt. That's where technique gets you, my friend."

I respond, too loudly, "What are you doing? I don't get this. I have to tell you, you were both a lot more fun here last time. What gives?"

"Look, we're not stupid," Carlos says. "We know where this is heading. We want to see you stay. You need a community like this, man. But we can't talk you into it. See, what Andy's giving you is so much bigger than you can know. You have no idea what the old guy's handing you. You can't see it. You're still too proud."

Suddenly he slaps his hands together, shaking his head in frustration, "Aaargh! I'm doing it again. I'm sorry, man. You don't need Carlos poking at you."

"No, just say it, Carlos. You want to say something to me, just say it." I'm really agitated now.

Carlos sits back in his chair. "You want me to, then I will. Do you mind an observation, Steven?"

"I'm not sure." I shake my head and cross my arms. "I don't get you guys. You talk about this being a 'safe place,' but neither of you two seem very safe at the moment."

Carlos puts his fork down and pats his hands on his knees, like he's realizing the need to change his approach.

"I guess that depends on what you mean by safe, huh?" he says. "See, man, if safe is just nice and sweet, where everybody's smiling at you and nobody's ever dealing with nothing, that's not safe. That's a retirement home. I like nice. Even Hank likes nice. Push come to shove, nice wins. But nice ain't enough for safe. A safe place isn't a soft place.

"Safe is a place where you can get out the worst about you and they don't run you off, talk you down, or head for the hills. It's having someone to stand with when you start to face the shameful stuff, man. It's where you can be a jerk and still have a place at the table the next day…where you don't have to hide or fake or pretend or bluff. Safe is being loved *more* for revealing your crap, not less. Safe is not having to 'man up' or be coerced to 'get real' or none of that nonsense."

"No kidding," Hank adds. "Nothing worse than a bunch of guys in the name of 'being real' trying to one-up each other with their Internet porn issues or how much they drink. It's almost like bragging that you're a real man. Really, just another form of hiding. Because you ain't giving anyone in that room permission to help and stand with you in the issue. Dumb game. Fake game."

"See," Carlos says, "the deal isn't being able to just let everybody hear your garbage. Who wants that? Who needs that? I can get that in my own head. Safe is where I can tell you my garbage so you can enter in and stand with me in the solution of it. That's safe, man."

Hank, reaching over and spearing another piece of shrimp off my plate, says, "You gonna eat that? You don't wanna eat seafood after it's been sitting out this long. Let me take the hit. An important guy like yourself, you can't be risking salmonella."

I regroup. "All right, Carlos, I'm ready for your observation."

"All right. This relational solution stuff, the good stuff? Well, it's messy, man. Because it demands that you care about something more than getting better before you can ever get better."

I blurt out, "Do you know how stupid that sounds?"

Hank wipes his mouth with his napkin and then says slowly and loudly enough for others to hear, "Do you know how lame your game plan has been for us to watch?"

The table and the entire deck are uncomfortably quiet.

Carlos puts his hand on my arm. "Forgive my knuckle-dragging friend. See why I don't take him out much?" Carlos gives a look that tells Hank he'll take it from here. "But embedded in his primordial rudeness is straight-on truth. You know what you're trying to do?"

I stare at him blankly. It's taking a lot of effort to stay in my chair right now.

"No, you don't. So let me tell you. You're trying to make

it look like you're giving Andy a way in. But you won't open any of the locks. You're trying to give permission to *something about you* but not to *you*. You get that? And man, that's only an elaborate attempt to solve an issue with a newer technique. It'll work about as good as your last twelve. It's like some kind of twisted manifest destiny, you know? You don't allow it to work and then blame it for not working. So you go back to your old stuff and think you're back in control. Am I close?"

I pull my lips in and stare at him, resisting giving him any satisfaction.

"But see, the other option is *real* scary, huh?"

"Steven, you ever get a toothache?" he asks. "No way you're going to no dentist, right? We know what that's all about. Needles in your gums and people with their hands inside your mouth. But this toothache, it's more pain than you can bear. So you search around the house till you find some Anbesol or something. You rub it in, and boom, the pain goes down. And you go on your way, able to convince yourself that you won't have that pain again. But you got an abscess growing in there, man! It's not going away because you rub some brand-name ointment from Walgreen's on it. You get what I'm saying?"

He's talking a mile a minute again. I can barely keep up.

"Steven, I gotta tell you, man, it's real hard to watch someone cover pain with something that makes them hurt even more. Until you go to a dentist, you've got a black, rotting jaw just waiting to blow up."

"Okay," Hank says, pretending nausea, "*now* who's messing with people's appetites?"

These guys sound a lot better when Andy's around. Hank's getting under my skin. And Carlos's whole patronizing dialect is starting to wear thin. I'm beginning to wonder what Andy sees in these guys. My thought is interrupted by Carlos's cell phone. It's Andy. He's been delayed and won't be able to make it for lunch. I immediately plan a polite exit.

Hank smiles knowingly. "Well, you need to go now, don't you?"

"What?" I feign.

Carlos says, "It's fine, man. It's all good. Hank and me, we're like an acquired taste. We're like wasabi. You ever had wasabi? Really good with some soy sauce and a California roll. But you don't wanna be eating it straight. Your eyes water, and you wish you'd never been born. That's how Hank and I seem to affect folks. An hour around us, and people are wishing they'd never been born."

Carlos smiles at me as he reaches for his drink. "So maybe we'll see you next time, when you come back with the California roll, eh?"

I put down cash for my food and begin to excuse myself.

"I feel like I should pay for your meal because I ate so much of it," Hank says, patting his stomach. "I'm not going to, but I thought it would be nice to tell you that."

This guy is a real piece of work.

Hank nods his head toward me. "Hey, one more thing. Don't leave yet."

I sit back down.

"I'm gonna say this because I'm not sure I'm going to see you again."

*He may not be far off there.* "Why would you say that, Hank?" I ask.

Ignoring my feigned confusion, Hank says, "Andy had to sell the car."

"What? The *Electra*? Andy sold the Electra?"

"Yep, " he answers, looking away.

"Why would he sell it?"

"Long story."

"Why didn't he tell me?" I ask.

Hank continues, still looking away. "A young guy he knows from church lost his job. He has a wife and three young kids. One of those middle-management cutback stories. They were about to lose their home. So Andy makes some phone calls and gets him a position in the same industry. But the guy's still too far behind to keep his house. So Andy sells the car. Gets a bunch for it. Covers almost the whole nut. None of us would have known except the guy's wife shows up here one day last week, looking for Andy, to thank him. She tells Carlos, Cynthia, and me the whole story.... That old cat, he's something."

"But he loved that car," I say, standing up. "I don't think I've ever seen someone enjoy something as much as he did that car."

"Yeah, a lot of us have taken a lot of drives with the old cat in that wagon."

I'm still stunned. "I don't get it. Why would he give that car up when it was used for so much good?"

"Maybe," Hank says, turning to look at me, "he wasn't so sure it still was."

I don't know what to say. I sit back down. Carlos is quiet, letting Hank handle this.

"Look, Steven, you haven't done anything wrong to me. So forgive me if what I say doesn't fit. In my work I get to see a lot of sharp young guys on the move. See 'em all the time. They blow through, and mostly just use people to get somewhere else. They pretend interest. They make you think they really did want to have lunch with you. And then, when they get what they want, or discover what they want isn't there, they're gone. I feel like I can size 'em up before they hit the front door. That may not be fair, but I'm usually pretty accurate."

Hank takes a long pause and then says, "So I just want to tell you to be kind to Andy when you walk out. He really cares for you. See, after you leave, we're the ones who have to clean up."

He stares into my eyes for an uncomfortably long time.

"Well, thanks for the shrimp." He nods. "Have a good day."

I'm embarrassed and angry all at once. I'm not sure what to say. I want to say something that'll put Hank in his place, justify myself, and allow me to leave with the final word. But nothing comes. So I get up, mumble something about the check, and walk out of the restaurant.

# "This Whole Stinking Thing's a Joke!"

*(Tuesday Evening, April 14)*

"This whole stinking thing's a joke!" I yell out loud in my car as I speed out of Bo's parking lot. I fly down Lincoln, with music on louder than usual, making all the lights. *I am so sick of this.* Within several minutes I am in the Marriott's fitness center, replaying this insane last month over and over, underscored by the sound of my feet pounding on a treadmill.

*I don't know what I'm supposed to do. I'm trying crap I'd usually mock just to convince my wife that I hear her. For what? I think she's actually liking that I'm out here in a hotel. Everybody's winning at my expense. I'm giving a bunch of wannabes a chance to work me over for being successful. Those guys all sit around with free time on a Thursday because they can't do what I can. And then I let them demean me. "Steven, you're too proud. Steven, you don't let anyone in. Steven, you think you've got all the answers. Steven, you don't give permission. Steven, you're angry."*

*How about, "Hank, you're in a dead-end job. Carlos, you talk too much and you cover for your stupid friend Hank too much. Cynthia, you get too close to people's faces. Andy . . . you're an idiot for selling that car. . . ."*

*So, why can't someone who does things well just be recognized as better? Can't Tiger Woods admit he's the best golfer in the world? Would that be too superior? I have to go into therapy because everyone else has issues and I'm supposed to be sensitive to the fact that they're weaker? Why should I have to pretend I'm a failure like everyone else?*

The speed of my argument with myself is matching my increasing speed on the machine. Forty minutes later, I'm still angry and now tired as well. I get off and make my way up to my room.

I find myself sitting on the floor leaning against the front of the bed, pulling off wet socks while positioning a towel between the bed and my head. I am still angry. I eventually get up to look on the counter, hoping to see a new batch of oranges. I think I finished off the last one yesterday. But there's nothing. Someone even took the bowl away.

*Great. I've got to work in a new housekeeping team. . . . I gotta get out of here. I'm obsessing over oranges.*

I walk over to my "workstation" and sit down in the ergonomic work chair the hotel is touting these days. I stare out the window at the parking garage that has been my view for the last month. Off in the distance there is the annoying beeping of construction equipment moving back and forth. I have convinced myself I somehow deserve this view.

"Thirty-three days. I've been living in a hotel room for thirty-three days." I am surprised I said those last words out loud. "And who am I talking to? You? Then listen to me. I'm sick of this. I feel like I'm performing for You too, and You're either not paying attention or You're siding with Carlos and Hank. And I'm done with it.

"You know what I think about when I lie here in bed and can't sleep? Of course You do. I've been looking over the last decade and asking: Has there been any proof that You've helped in anything I've accomplished? Anything I couldn't have done without Your help? Is there any evidence that You've caused my success, my promotions, my advancement? I haven't asked for Your help, and You haven't given it. But in the one area I've asked, *my relationship with my wife,* You haven't done squat. You've left me out, alone, in a hotel, playing the fool. I know I'm gonna pay for this; I know You hold all the cards. But I gotta say, either this whole God thing has been made up in our heads, or You're not quite as powerful as You've been advertised."

I get up and walk out of the room and down to my car, to drive to a restaurant so I can, once again, eat alone.

# Good-bye to the Mint-Strawberry Water

*(Saturday Morning, April 18)*

Well, today I say good-bye to the people calling me "sir," to the view of the parking garage and the oil painting of fruit in room 643. Others will watch *me* check out today. Thirty-seven days. I think only Howard Hughes beats that total. No more mint-and-strawberry-infused water for me. Today I am going home.

Lindsey called just minutes ago. She was crying, asking me if I'd like to come home. I know not everything is solved. I know we will hit glitches. I know I can often be a lot of work. But it is time. We are husband and wife and we are a family. I have to run down to San Diego today to preview some software at a convention, but tonight I'll sleep in my own bed.

I want to call Andy and thank him for all he's done. But I've ignored his last half dozen e-mails. I don't want to deal with that right now. He'll figure it out. I'll call him sometime soon. But this whole strange season just ended five minutes ago. I'm going home.

It's after eleven when I pull up again into our driveway. I turn off the car and remember the last evening I sat out here like this. A lot has changed. I don't think we'll ever repeat that night. I feel so much better than I did four nights ago, when I was angry at the world. I was getting so worn down by it all.

The lights are out in the house. I still don't have a key. She even changed the code to the garage opener. So I leave my car out in the driveway and use the front door, which she said she'd leave unlocked. As I step into the house I see a flickering light coming from the family room. I walk in to find Jennifer, asleep on the couch, in the dark, with the TV on.

I quietly call out, "Hey, kid."

"Hey, Dad," she mumbles as she sits up. "I think I fell asleep."

I sit down next to her. "So what were you watching?"

"I'm not sure. Some reality show rerun or something."

"You're up pretty late."

"Yeah. I'm just waiting for a shirt to dry. Then I'm off to bed."

We're both quiet for a few moments.

"Glad you're home, Dad," she says, staring at the television.

"Thanks."

I want to touch her hand, but I don't. Jennifer doesn't show or allow a lot of affection.

"Mom's been asleep for a while."

"Thanks."

As I get up to leave the room, Jennifer's voice stops me.

"Hey, Dad?"

"Yeah?"

"You know that I could hear your fight with Mom that night, right?"

"Yeah, I've been meaning to talk to you about that. The time just never seems right."

"That's all right," she says. "Mom and I talked."

"Good." I stand there waiting for more.

"So, I just wanted to say that we should all be nice to each other now, you know?"

"Yeah. We all want that, kid. I think it's going to be better now."

"Yeah."

My daughter is staring at the television. But I know she's not watching it. She's like her dad. She has a hard time letting anyone see what's going on inside. So she acts like she doesn't care. But I know the things she's saying right now are hard for her. I don't think she's ever tried to say these things to me before. How scary is this for her? She's only eleven and feels like she has to help teach her parents how to get along.

"Dad?"

"Yeah?"

"Be nice to Mom. She really loves you a lot."

"I know. I'm trying to learn to not be such a jerk."

"You're not a jerk, Dad."

"Thanks, Jenny."

She turns off the television. I start to leave the room. From the dark I hear her voice.

"Don't get divorced, okay?"

Through the darkness, I answer back, "Don't worry, honey. Nobody's going to get divorced. Now get to bed, kid."

As she leaves the room and begins to climb the stairs, I follow her out and whisper to her, "You know I love you a lot, right?"

"Yeah. I love you too, Dad."

# Just Alan

*(Wednesday Morning, May 6)*

It's been a couple of weeks since I moved back home. And I'd have to say it's been going well. It does feel like we're being pretty careful around one another. All three of us are just finding our way back to each other. We're trying to do more stuff together, as a family. Last night, I got home around five and we packed a picnic dinner and rode bikes to the beach. We put a blanket on the sand, and the three of us watched the sun go down as we ate chicken. Pretty cool. I missed this.

It's five forty-five, Friday morning. I'm blindly negotiating my way down the stairs, hoping Lindsey made coffee. I hear an unfamiliar voice coming from the kitchen. As I get closer I realize that Lindsey is listening to our answering machine. I stop on the last step of the stairs.

*"Lindsey, I just wanted to say that I really enjoyed our talk yesterday. I'm looking forward to continuing it today."*

I stand in the dark, not sure what I've just heard. By the time I walk into the kitchen, my wife is leaning on the counter at the answering machine, replaying the message. She is unaware I am in the room.

*"Lindsey, I just wanted to say that I really enjoyed our talk yesterday. I'm looking forward to continuing it today."*

I wait until the message is over. She is staring at the machine.

"Who was that?" I ask.

"What? Oh, just someone." She's clearly startled.

"Who?"

She doesn't look me in the eye. "Just Alan. He's the counselor I was telling you about before. Remember?"

That sick feeling in my stomach returns, the way it did a few weeks ago when Lindsey mentioned him.

"Lindsey, why is he calling you?"

She heaves that sigh she makes when she thinks I'm getting out of control. *I'm not.*

"I was looking for some perspective from him a while back, remember? Then he asked me for help with his daughter. That's all."

"A married man doesn't call a married woman to tell her he hopes to see her again."

"That's not what he— Steven, please. It's nothing."

My voice goes up. "No, Lindsey. It's not."

"It *is* nothing. He's just a friend. Okay? He's just someone I talk to, along with half a dozen others at the gym. *You* talk to people."

I shake my head. "Why are you getting defensive?"

"Please stop this. You're doing it again. You've got that rigid face again. Please, just stop and listen."

I'm right on this. She's trying to spin out of this. I know there's something more. *Just say it.*

"I'll listen," I bark, "when you start making sense."

She steadies herself, like she's resigned to have to fight this one out. I can see she's as frustrated as I am.

"Well, then try this: Steven, I'm not sure if it's dawned on you yet, but I'm a social person. I've got a whole bunch of things inside me to talk about, almost all the time. You're usually so preoccupied that I don't get a chance to say many of them. Ask your daughter. She talks to me all the time. And you wonder why you can't get her to say boo to you about her day at school. She knows you're not available and has learned to not bother."

Lindsey walks over to the kitchen sink. "Women just need to talk more. And some men get that. That's all this is—just a male friend who doesn't mind talking. What about that is defensiveness?"

"Lindsey, do you realize that every time I say something you don't like, you pull the 'Steven-is-preoccupied' card? Every time."

She spins around from the sink. "Do you realize that every time I pull the 'Steven-is-preoccupied' card, it's because you are?"

"That's so stupidly unfair. It's not true and it's unfair."

"Steven, I'm wanting you to take a deep breath. If you want to have a conversation, we can have a conversation. But this is not a conversation. This is the freaked-out guy about to lose it. Now, you're going to get angry in a minute and say a bunch of things you'll wish you hadn't. And then I'm going to walk out that door and drive somewhere. Then I'm going to call you on my cell phone to tell you that this is not working and that I cannot keep doing this. And you're going to be very sorry, and it's going to be very strange for a long time. Or we can stop right now, and I'll hand you a cup of coffee and you can wake up and remember to stop being a control freak and we can just go on."

"You know what? You can bag the righteous indignation speech, Lindsey. You're hiding something!" I say, almost yelling. "You give a lecture and then I'm supposed to just be quiet because I get angry, while you go live your double life."

"You are so out of control, again."

"Then go! I'm sick of this."

"Shut up, Steven. You're gonna wake her up."

"You shut up! I've done everything right. And you've been seeing some shrink guy while I'm living in a hotel."

"Get out of this house, Steven. I'm not leaving, you are."

"I'm not doing that again. This is my house. You can go live with your boyfriend!"

She screams as loud as I've ever heard anyone scream: "Get out! Get out! *Get OUT!*"

She runs over to the phone.

I yell, "What are you doing? Who are you calling?"

"The police. I'm calling the police! Get out of this house now!"

She's screaming and crying at the same time. I hear Jennifer's door open.

"Mom? What's going on?"

And I run out of the house.

Within seconds I'm in my car, headed north. I don't know where to go. I find myself driving up into the hills overlooking the ocean. I park my car in the same area Andy first brought me. A thousand screaming explosions are crashing around my head. I'm still shaking.

*I did it again. I lost it. What have I done? Should I call her? What if she was right? What if that was all it was with this guy?*

I sit there, limp, knowing I've been here so many times before. And every time, I promise I'll guard myself from allowing it to happen again. The pitiful part is that I actually believe I will. Still breathing hard, staring out across the valley where my whole world is free-falling into chaos, I'm struck with the thought that this all may not get better. That I don't have the ability to fix myself and that Lindsey and Jennifer will continue to suffer for it. Why does she stay? Maybe this time she won't.

*What do I do?*

*God, what is wrong with me? My marriage is falling apart. I freaked out again. I keep scaring this woman who used to be all I could think about. Please help me. I don't know what to do anymore. I'm so afraid I'll always be like this. Help me.* My head drops into my hands. *Do You hear me? Help me. Please. Help me.*

After a few minutes, I lift my head and stare. What comes next? I've been through this drill with her so many times.

One of us gets into a car and drives in no particular direction—usually her. Then I feel lousy all day. Then sometime this evening or tomorrow morning, I'll sit down in front of Lindsey and apologize. It's like clockwork. I'll own everything, even though I don't believe it. I'm just wanting things back to...whatever they were before. I'll ask her to forgive me. I'll send flowers. I'll write notes. What a putz! I'm like an actor in a soap opera trying to schmooze my way back to normalcy.

The saddest part is that Lindsey has also learned to play the game. She's found her role in this madness. So far, she's loved me enough to keep forgiving me. She tries to forget and pretend it'll get better.

So why does it feel different now?

I'm onto myself, that's why. Have I ever thought that before? I no longer trust my own remorse. All these years, I've apologized for my crappy behavior. But I was never sorry, not really. I gave myself so much arrogant license to hurt her and anyone else. Because I was bigger and stronger. And they were weaker.

*Oh, God. I've been lying to myself. How do I get out of this? I just want to start all over, throw away everything. Please help me. I don't know if I can do this. Please help me start over.*

Eventually, I get up and drive back down the hill, past east Culver City, past Venice, then past Marina del Rey, all the way back to our home in Manhattan Beach. I turn onto our street, but Lindsey's car is gone. I call her cell phone...then again. No answer.

I don't leave a message.

# "I'm a Mess, Andy."

*(Friday Morning, May 8)*

Sitting in my driveway, I become overwhelmed by the realization of what I've risked. I look in the rearview mirror. My hair is an oily mess, my mouth feels like chalk, and I need a shave. The *Wall Street Journal* should get a look at me now.

I am suddenly struck with this thought: *I have no one to talk to about this . . . except Andy. I'm not sure what he'll do with it, but I have to call him.*

I quickly remember I've erased his messages and don't have his number in my phone. My mind is spinning. I run inside the house, change out of my pajamas into some clothes I find lying on the floor, and jump back into the car. I drive to Bo's, which is not yet open. But Bo is out front signing for a delivery. He's ready to banter with me but does a double take when he sees my condition.

"Who you be needin' *cher*?"

I tell him I'm looking for Andy.

Bo gives me the address for a dock in Marina del Rey. It's the same marina where my CEO's boat is moored. I'm ashamed to think of how many times I've been in and out of that marina and never even noticed the man who has become so important to me.

It's about a mile and a half away. I start walking fast, sensing an urgency to solve something before any more damage is done. I've walked more than halfway before it dawns on me that I drove my car to Bo's.

I continue walking anyway.

It's 9:00 a.m. by the time I reach the marina. I run down the walkway to where the boats are docked. Andy is nowhere in sight. I yell his name a couple of times. Nothing. Exhausted and overwhelmed, I collapse onto a bench. The sun is glaring intensely off the water. I feel like I'm hungover.

I have no idea how much time has passed when I hear a voice.

"Are you here for your boat, sir?"

I answer back without looking up, "No, thanks. I'm just sitting."

"Well, look, fella, we don't allow loitering here."

I look up to see Andy. He's grinning at me.

I smile weakly.

"Gotcha...," he says.

He's in his usual Hawaiian shirt, cargo shorts, flip-flops, and sunglasses. He's holding two steaming paper cups of coffee.

"Bo called and told me you might be stopping by. Hey, you look terrible. What, is it Hobo Day down at the office?"

I look down at what I'm wearing. In my hurry back at the house, I'd pulled on the clothes I wore to paint the bathroom the day before. I've been walking through the Marina del Rey yachting community in slippers, blue jeans, and a cutoff sweatshirt spattered in purple and aqua.... Nice.

I gratefully reach for the cup of coffee. "Andy, how many times have you checked out the boat for our group?"

"Oh, a few times or so. Cool yacht."

"You knew who I was back then?"

No response. He sits down on the bench next to me. Just

having something warm in my hands feels good . . . feels real. Like life is actually happening.

"I'm a mess, Andy."

"Well, at least you haven't lost your keen sense of the obvious." He pats my knee playfully.

"Andy, I'm sorry," I say. "I'm really sorry. I haven't called you or returned your calls or e-mails. But I really need to talk to you."

Before answering, Andy blows on his coffee a long time. "Uh-huh. Well, you see, I think I'm gonna have to say no to that."

"What?" I nearly choke on the sip I've just taken.

"I've got some boats to clean, and I think maybe I'm not the best person to walk this through with you."

"Are you kidding me?" I say. "I think you're the *only* person who can walk this through with me."

"Well, see, that's gonna be a problem." He is still blowing on his coffee, staring straight ahead.

I turn slightly toward him. "Andy, when I didn't get back to you, I really messed up, didn't I?"

Andy stands up and walks to the rail overlooking the boats and the harbor. He is turned away from me as he speaks.

"I was keeping up with you through your dad long before we met at Fenton's. I've cared about you for some time now. I'd rehearsed a dozen times what I'd say if we ever got the chance to talk. Many times I wanted to introduce myself to you here at the marina, but the time was never right. So when I finally got the chance to be in your life, maybe it was too important to me that you'd let me in. I've thought a lot about that these last few weeks."

I sit, staring at him, unable to think of something appropriate to say. Eventually I break the silence.

"I don't know about any of that, Andy. I just know this

isn't about you. *You* didn't do anything wrong. It's all been about me. Hank warned me I would do this very thing. That I would leave you, reject you. I don't think you can know how much I hate admitting he was right, but he was. He saw where I was headed."

I stand up and face him. I can't look him in the eye for long, so I begin pacing. I'm really scared. My hands are sweating. I start trying to say words, but nothing comes. Finally, I catch my breath and mumble more than speak, still not able to look at him directly.

"I don't know what to say, Andy. I'm so sorry. This was all new to me, and I didn't know what to do with it. I don't let people in like this. I never have. It got too close. So I ran. I run a lot."

I stop and look at him again until he is looking into my eyes.

"I know this sounds weak, but I do need you, Andy. I'm in a lot of trouble. I hurt Lindsey. I really screwed up again. I don't know where to go if you won't talk to me."

He peers back at me, his face expressionless.

"Andy, are you gonna say something, or are you gonna just let me stew here?"

Still nothing. I catch a glance from him, just long enough to give a hint of a smile.

"Look, Andy," I say in a voice that sounds far more serious than I expected it to. "I'm not leaving. So you've got a choice. It's not going to look good to your boss if some homeless guy keeps moping around the marina. And I *will* mope. I'll make a scene and throw your name around like confetti. I didn't get where I am by being passive."

I take a couple of steps toward him. "Look, I'll help you clean boats. I don't think anyone will notice."

He sips his coffee and takes a long look at my clothing. He smiles.

"Well, you *would* blend in. In that outfit, you should probably start with the bilge pumps."

I smile. "I deserve that."

"You do." He sighs. "Let's get to work."

He turns and heads down the walkway without another word, and I follow.

Over the next several hours, Andy and I wash down boats together. He familiarizes me with the bilge pump on several of them. I tell him everything that has just happened, leaving nothing out, including my pleading with God and my realizations of how I've hurt my wife.

When we finish, we climb to the deck of the boat we've just finished. He looks out at the harbor for a while before speaking.

"Let me see if I've got this right," Andy says, stroking his chin. "You said these words to your wife: 'You shut up! I've done everything right. And you've been seeing some shrink guy while I'm living in a hotel.' Then you felt that wasn't enough and added, 'This is my house. You can live with your boyfriend!' And then you ran out the door. Do I have that right?"

It sounds really awful coming out of his mouth. "Yeah. Not exactly in that order, but, yeah. . . ."

"Whooeee. And I'm the one checking out boats while you're getting profiled in the *Wall Street Journal*? Where's the justice in *that* universe?"

I shake my head. "I guess I deserve that too, don't I?"

"Yes, you do."

He pulls a cigar out of his shirt pocket, cuts off the end, and lights it. Then he looks at me and says, "Well, Steven, looks like we're not in Kansas anymore."

"What's that supposed to mean?"

"I don't know if you've noticed," Andy replies, "but I

haven't really done much thus far to address the issues you've confided to me."

"Oh, it's crossed my mind on occasion," I say.

"Would you like to know why?"

"Yes, that *would* be nice."

He blows out a puff of smoke. "You weren't ready. And now, well, now you are."

"Let me get this right. I cause my wife to scream and call the police, and that makes me ready?"

He tilts his head a little. "Not exactly. The rage, damage, and remorse cycle—you've been there before."

"Yeah." I chuckle weakly. "A few times."

"And in the past, when the anger cooled down, you were always sad for the things you'd done. But today, humility has entered the picture. I'm nearly certain of it."

"How do you know that?"

"Two ways." He places the cigar in his mouth and holds up two fingers. "Today, for the first time, you're owning up to something deeper than your behavior."

I'm listening closely, waiting for a punch line.

"Did you catch that? That's huge. It's like two-thirds of the pie right there. You're owning the fact that you try to control others with your anger. This isn't just about fixing your anger. This is about who you are, why you do what you do. The difference couldn't be bigger."

I raise my hand. "Could you repeat that last sentence, the one about controlling others?"

"You're owning the consent you give yourself to control others with your anger."

"That's what I thought you said... and you're saying that's a big deal."

He nods. "Second way I know is that today you're trusting me with *you*. Up until now you were just negotiating whether you would trust me with your anger. That's playing with house money. It doesn't cost you much. And it sure isn't humility. Humility is trusting God and others with *you*—your whole person. If I'm not mistaken, that's what you're doing here. You're giving me access to *you*."

He takes out his cigar and points at my chest, smiling. Finally, he gets up and walks right up next to me. Like Cynthia, he's standing very close. Looking deeply into my eyes he says, "My young friend, we've finally shown up at the right address at the right time. This moment couldn't be rushed, coerced, or manipulated. We couldn't have found a shortcut to this moment. But now we're ready to play for real money.

"This is a sacred moment, my friend. With your permission, I have the privilege of protecting you."

I get up and pace the deck.

"I don't get it. You were just waiting for me to break down? Why didn't we just dive in and get to the root of my anger? Maybe I wouldn't have blown it again."

"Well, first of all, we were diving in. We were working at building a relationship where you could trust me. And all along you were learning about what you were missing in your own world. And until you figured that out and knew you could trust me, it wouldn't have worked. Like I said before, I could've given you answers, but you needed a foundation first. A foundation of grace."

We're standing side by side and he's looking at me, like, I don't know. Like he's looking for something behind my eyes. I can't remember anyone in my life talking like this to me. It feels good.

"But to fully answer your question," he says, turning back toward the ocean, "that'll demand some deeper explanation. Has the coffee kicked in?"

I shake my head back and forth, like a man trying to shake off drunkenness. "I hope so."

"Just sit back and let the old sea captain work."

I settle onto a bench and set my half-empty cup next to me.

"You heard of shame?"

"Shame," I repeat.

He nods. "Everyone eventually stumbles into the ugly experience called shame." He starts walking back and forth, working the deck like it belongs to him. "It's like in that dream where you're walking around naked. You know what I mean?"

"I hate that dream," I say.

"It's the worst. Maybe not as bad as the clown chasing me with a hatchet, but pretty close. You know that one? Or where you're trying to run but your feet won't move?"

"You're interrupting yourself."

"Right. So we experience shame hundreds of times before we reach adulthood. Maybe you get humiliated at a school dance. Maybe a coach rips you apart in front of your PE class. Or, you walk into a party and find your girlfriend making out with some guy from another school. Or maybe someone violates you—so badly you become convinced you can never tell anyone about it. People will tell you they don't carry any shame, but they do."

Andy looks at me. "You follow?"

"Perfectly. Brenda Magnusson, homecoming dance, 1991."

"Doesn't matter how competent, intelligent, or accomplished you are. You've got it tucked away in there. And nobody can cope for any great period of time with the feeling of that nakedness. You know what shame does? It takes a particular violation or several violations from your past, something that really got to you, and convinces you the person you felt like in that violation is who you'll always be, for the rest of your life. Sad, huh?"

"Yeah," I say, looking past him.

"So we fashion some fig leaves to protect ourselves. A manufactured story we create that we think will protect us from feeling that shame, so others don't see that nakedness in us. We don't want others to see us for the person the lie has told us we are. So we almost unconsciously create a lie to protect us from the lie. Bad combination."

"Slow down a minute. 'We don't want others to see us for the person the lie has told us we are.' Is that me?"

"We gradually learn to falsely rewrite our own story. We perfect a manipulated story, either of our own inferiority, superiority, or some pretty schizophrenic combination of the two. It becomes the lens we see our lives through. Folks who feel *inferior,* well, they blame themselves a lot and see themselves as the reason for most of their trouble...and the war in Vietnam. Now, someone who feels *superior,* he blames others and sees *them* as the reason for all his problems...and the war in Vietnam. Both are based in a lie. The inferior guy, you feel bad for. The superior guy—he's a lot of work. He usually thinks his problems are his wife or his coworkers or the guy in front of him in traffic. He doesn't need much of anything from anyone."

Suddenly, he stops like he's realized something.

"Yes, that's me," I say.

"Oh," he says, blinking as if just remembering where he is. "I wouldn't, well, uhm...yes. It's you. Perfect example."

"I get the point."

He clears his throat. "Now, the engine for every distorted behavior, like, say, anger, for example, is this central lie we've used to rewrite our story. And unfortunately, it only perpetuates and reenergizes our shame. It may go underground for a while, but it never goes away. And the saddest part is that it never does what we hope it will. It never covers the shame.

And it certainly never solves it. It can make us feel more presentable, but it does nothing to solve our condition. And meanwhile, everyone around us is aware of it and is being wounded by a man who feels relatively presentable."

"I take it this isn't supposed to be making me feel any better."

"Nope." Andy lifts one hand, motioning for me to stop talking. "But you were wanting me to fix your shame-fueled anger without giving me access to you and your superiority story."

"I was, huh?"

"You were just trying to modify bad behavior enough to keep you from getting thrown out of your house again... I'm just saying."

I shrug.

"See, I knew that game plan wouldn't work for you any more than it ever worked for me. Only a real friend would ever be allowed to address the shame driving your behavior."

His eyes search mine. "I think that's why you came here today... right?"

I think back to sitting in my driveway earlier, alone, without a hope in the world. "Yeah," I say. "That sounds a lot like why I'm here."

Andy suddenly gets a silly grin.

"Do you know what boat we're on right now?"

"Of course. This is our company's boat. I've sat on this bench many times."

Andy runs his hand across a stretch of rail. "Yep, a forty-five-foot princess. She gracefully houses twin turbo diesels and sexy new v-drives inside a state-of-the-art polished composite fiberglass hull. And she stables five hundred horses in each corral down below—horses that can fly in water. Inside she's dressed comfortably in European maple, full leather, and California Berber. She's trimmed out with a fifteen-foot beam and radar that can find a tugboat twenty-four miles away. And this sweetheart can dance at twenty knots before she's half a mile from the jetty. Twenty knots, my friend."

I look around the deck of the boat I thought I was so familiar with. "Wow. I'm impressed. I've never really paid much attention. I'm usually in the back, schmoozing potential clients."

"Part of my job as dockmaster," he says, still slowly running his hands along the rails, "is to check out the yachts. But on the side I clean a few and keep the engines fresh. So I tool 'em around the bay a bit. It's almost like owning several dozen yachts. What do you say we take the lady out for a spin?"

"You're aware my life is in shambles, right?"

"Oh, yeah." He smiles at me. "We've established that, I think."

"And you really think we should . . . ?"

"Yep."

"All right. I'm not calling the shots today."

"Good."

I find a cushioned seat, sit back, and watch Andy walk the length of the boat, meticulously checking features I never knew existed. He unlashes ropes and sits down in the captain's chair to start her up. Responding smoothly with a deep, low growl, it's like she belongs to him.

Soon we're free from the slip and slowly idling our way through the rows and rows of yachts, toward the jetty.

This is like one of those moments you watch in a movie. The setting and circumstances are so funny and out-of-place, it's obvious they were prepared a long time ago. *I'm on my boss's yacht, being driven around by a crazy man in a ball cap, who's teaching me how to not end up like my boss.*

I laugh out loud. I imagine God smiling next to me,

slapping me on the back and saying, *"How's this for a Kodak moment, huh? You might want to listen to this guy. I've gone to quite a bit of trouble to get you here."*

It's all very peaceful. I hear mast bells lightly clanging in the breeze. Once again I'm enveloped by the low rumble of an engine steered by Andy. How can this be? I'm missing from work—nobody knows where I am, and, for the moment, I don't really care. In the hour of my greatest revealed failure, I'm enjoying the sea for the first time since I was a kid.

Andy picks up his speech where he left off, while maneuvering through the breakwater toward open sea. "Steven, many counselors are trained to help you work on a particular behavior. That's called behaviorism."

I make my way up closer to where Andy is so I can hear over the engine.

"Go ahead," I say.

"It's like an elaborate game of Whack-A-Mole. Moles pop out of holes, and you whack 'em with a mallet. You score points by how many moles you can whack in a certain amount of time. You're going along just fine for a while, racking up lots of points. But then the game starts speeding up. We think we've 'fixed' a behavior, and four more critters pop out. Eventually we're spending our entire time whacking moles. Therapists put their kids through college teaching us how to hit the little rodents quicker."

Andy looks up from the controls. "But no behavioral mallet can hit the shame that triggers the lie that releases the mole."

He lets that picture settle in for a time before continuing. "Now, other people will want to work on what they call your 'root behaviors.' That's psychology. You try to find your way back to some event in your early life. You uncover and examine events that help explain why you needed an inferiority or superiority story. And now the problems in your life will finally be solved. But a good psychologist will caution you that all you've done is identify the elements of and causes for your self-story. While that's incredibly helpful, and may feel good, it doesn't solve anything. Your shame remains unresolved. Because at the end of the day, no psychological mallet can solve the shame that triggers the lie that releases the mole."

His voice has gotten progressively louder. We're skimming along out into deeper water. I want to indicate that I'm following, but I don't think he could hear me, so I just keep squinting into the sun.

"Just about the time you've become totally disillusioned with your journey, Jesus will step out of the shadows and stand next to you. He'll look in your eyes and say, 'I took your shame for you two thousand years ago. And I won the right to have it never, ever again define you. It doesn't belong to you anymore. It's over. That's the truth.' "

"Is that the 'come to Jesus' card?"

"Yeah." He smiles. "I guess so."

"See, I gotta tell you. It's just too much magic for me. Too many mirrors, too much smoke."

He smiles again. "Humor me, will you?"

He's turned around in his captain's chair and is no longer steering.

I point. "Andy, you gonna . . . ?"

"Oh, yeah. Sorry." He turns and resumes steering.

"So why don't we experience that freedom, most of us?" he asks.

I look at him blankly.

"It's not a rhetorical question. If God took our shame away, then why doesn't everyone experience that freedom?"

"I guess I don't know."

Andy taps the steering wheel. "Well, it's not because we're

not sincere or educated enough. We haven't learned how to trust what He says is true about us. It's that simple. See, those nice theological concepts don't do much for you."

"I'll say."

"And it's not a matter of willpower or screwing yourself up to believe what you don't yet believe. It's just being willing to try on the new clothing. To think about what it would look like if you believed He really took the shame away. The person my shame has told me I am no longer needs to be listened to."

Something in what Andy is saying is beginning to make sense.

"Until we believe what Jesus says He did," Andy says, "it's hard to accept the lies we tell ourselves and replace them with the real identity God's handing us. He offers this new life, the life we were trying to fake our way to with our self-stories. And it comes without any condemnation. He's smiling, with His arm around us, looking at our messed-up lives together with us and saying He's crazy about us. Nothing surprises Him or makes Him want to run. He's known about our problems from before the world began, and He knows where we're headed now. And that flat-out trounces shame."

We've slowed to an idle in front of the huge ridge of stacked boulders that separates the jetty from the ocean.

"So Jesus asks us to trust Him, not fake it or perform for Him. Slowly we discover there are some others we can grow and introduce to that trust." He looks over at me. "Even a guy as screwed up as me can give a friend a safe place. Even a man as flawed as I am can help a friend rewrite his story with the real story, the true story—of *Christ coming through me*. That's who Steven Kerner is on his worst day."

He spins all the way around and says, "Now that dog, I'm telling you, that dog'll hunt."

"Okay. I'm starting to follow you," I say. "But you lost me when you said everyone has shame. I get that some people might live out of shame. But me? Maybe arrogance or pride. I haven't suffered ten minutes with shame my entire life."

"Then tell me this, Steven," he says, leaning forward. "What drives your need to be right all the time, to defeat anyone in your path? What drives you to overachieve? What keeps you beating yourself up for not performing to your high expectations? What keeps you comparing yourself with everyone, looking over your shoulder, and putting down others? Where does that come from if not a deep, innate fear that you aren't enough and others might see it? Only one condition motivates such behavior. It starts with the letter *s* and rhymes with *flame*."

I look up at him. "Okay, then you tell me this—why didn't this all get solved at the start when I became a Christian?"

"Great question."

Andy starts working his way back through the jetty, making big, slow circles as he speaks. "Steven, most of us think that once we believe in Jesus, we'll live magically ever after. Cashews and sweet corn will grow year-round in our front yards." He pauses. "Then we discover we still know very well how to hurt others and make crappy life choices. And this realization breaks our hearts. This is where the rewritten story kicks in. It whispers to us that we don't deserve such a life, that Jesus is fully disgusted with our failures. So, after beating ourselves up, we start trying to fix ourselves, reform, and relieve the disgust we presume He has for us. Welcome to much that passes as church. We play right into self-disgust. And many churches keep their crowds reminded that Jesus is fully disgusted with them. This is the greatest lie in the mix—the conviction that we can fix ourselves, the conviction that He wants us to try, the conviction that He's angry at us if we don't try harder."

"He doesn't want us to try to fix ourselves?"

"Steven, if we actually could fix ourselves, why would Jesus have had to die?"

I look at the deck and eventually hold up my palms.

"That whole feeling that I'm not enough, that there's something uniquely wrong in me? It gets dismantled the same way you first received grace—by accepting that you can't earn it. Wrap your head around this, Steven: He offers us an entirely new story—one with no condemnation, inferiority, inadequacy, or insecurity. No more trying to prove to anyone that I'm someone I know I'm not. Over. Done."

"This is *so* not what I'm used to hearing about God," I say. "Not at all."

Several yachts and smaller boats are slowly gliding out of slips and into the open harbor. The sun is now high enough to paint their wakes with shimmering gold and orange. It's incredibly beautiful out here. I've sat here so many times and never noticed it at all.

Andy interrupts my reflection. "Let me tell you what you've gotten yourself into. If you're honest, it feels really good to be cared for, to have someone stand with you in what's been freaking you out for decades."

I nod. "Yeah."

"But it's scary too. It's kind of like when we first begin to follow Him. We're really excited, but at some point we begin to wonder, *What's God gonna do with me now that I've given my life to Him?* We become afraid again, of the very One who has broken through our defenses to give us love.

"See, we're still convinced we're not really worth being loved. And our acceptance of grace is fragile and vulnerable. You're incredibly successful, Steven, but deep down you're convinced that you're not *worthy* of that success. You're not even worth being loved. So the thought of someone wanting to love you messes with your head, doesn't it?"

I'm looking out at the water, unable to respond to Andy quite yet.

"But you have to receive it. It's a lot different than trying to love others or God enough. It's learning to say, 'If God says I'm worthy of being loved, then I'm worthy. Forget what my old tapes tell me. I'm going with God's assessment.' "

"Okay," I say. "I think I can do that."

"It'll feel like you've opened Pandora's box. Because you know *you,* and all the garbage inside. And you're terrified someone else will now see it. But here's the difference—" Andy leans in even closer. "It won't matter to you anymore. If they see the truth about you, you'll actually be *happy* about it. You'll feel completely different about yourself from there on out. And that's because you'll see all your junk now only through God's eyes, through the eyes of *love,* not condemnation."

"So, I don't have to get there all at once, do I?"

"You kidding me?" He leans back and laughs. "Look at Peter. He changed in and out of his new identity more often than Bette Midler changed her wardrobe at a reunion concert."

I'm no longer listening to Andy as much as watching him. He's really enjoying himself. He's waited for this a long time.

A breeze has picked up from the direction of the ocean. The boats in the marina are bobbing and creaking as we talk, as if happy to be here.

"Andy, since the moment we met, I've been asking myself why you're doing this. Was I a project? Were you doing a favor for my dad, or what? You know what I think now?"

He stares at me.

"I think you wanted a friend. I think you wanted to care about me."

"I do. I really do. I care about you a lot. Why else would I drive around with an arrogant jerk who thinks my sunglasses look stupid?"

"Not stupid." I smile. "They just make you look like, well, an old guy."

He laughs hard. "Steven, look at me. I *am* an old guy. I was watching *The Ed Sullivan Show* the evening he introduced the Beatles to America."

"On *what* show?" I've heard of the show, but it feels good playing him a little.

Andy looks at me with annoyance and pity.

"Besides," he says, "today's sunglasses cost too much, and they make you look like a bug."

Andy pulls on the rope of a bell above his head, for no apparent reason.

"Yes. God has given me a real care and love for you, whether or not you ever figure out how to receive it. Whether or not you ever figure out how to love or be loved by your wife. I'm going to be your friend. I want to stand with you."

"I think I always felt if I let someone too close, they'd have something on me, leverage or control."

"Control is an expression of superiority," he says, "always using the power of position and title. That's why you withhold permission from everyone. But protection is an expression of love."

"So you're saying I'll get there," I say.

"Pretty much. And have you noticed, we barely talk about symptoms anymore? You don't still think the goal is to fix you, do you?"

"I guess not."

"Pretty cool, huh?"

I nod. "Unless you have a wife somewhere in L.A. contemplating divorce."

"Patience, my friend," he says. "My guess is she's contemplated divorce before today."

I chuckle. "Thanks for the encouragement."

He relights his cigar and starts puffing away again. "Okay, okay. Stay focused. I'm actually working toward a point here. One more thing that protective love does—it creates vulnerability. My guess is you never imagined sharing the stuff that's been coming out of you these last few hours. That's why this is never about technique, never about 'five things to get someone to open up.' I never had a plan with you. I just wanted to allow this vulnerability to come out. My friend, this truth alone, being lived out, is going to turn your marriage upside down."

"What do you mean?" I ask.

"Well, I think you've been sad over what you've done a thousand times before. You've been sad that you got revealed, that you hurt Lindsey. I think you've felt *lots* of sadness, even remorse. But this might be the first time you've been able to face that it's more than a behavioral problem—you're actually admitting you use anger to control your world."

"Stop," I say. "I said that?"

"I believe you did."

I think for a moment. "Okay. I can see that. It just sounds like a pretty big deal when I hear you say it that way."

"And you're also discovering that you don't know how to stop it. For the first time, you can take those truths and offer them to God and to Lindsey. You get to really repent this time. Do you understand that? Repentance?"

I'm caught off guard, still thinking about my anger as a tool to control. "Uh, sure. Repentance. That's when you stop doing what you've been doing wrong and turn a 180. Right?"

He scrunches up his face. "Well, isn't that special?" Then, with mock sincerity he says, "Gee, I don't know why we didn't just do this before. Just stop doing what you've been doing wrong. Well, by golly, let's get right to that. What do you say?" He slaps his knee for mock emphasis.

I glare back at him. "Well, here's another time when you make what I say sound stupid."

"Yeah, I might be doing that. It's just that those tired, mindless clichés are part of the thinking that got you into this mess in the first place. Steven, don't you think if you could stop doing what you've been doing wrong, you'd have fixed things by now?"

I shrug with growing frustration. "I don't know what you want to hear, Andy. I'm back in junior high and the science teacher is looking for a specific answer. Why don't you just tell me, and then I'll know and we can move on?"

"I remind you of your science teacher in junior high?"

"Sometimes."

"Did he have those little white balls of spit at the edges of his mouth?"

"Yeah."

"Fair enough," he says. "It's just that when I give you the answer, you presume you get it, that you have it all figured out. I want you to get it on your own so you'll see that what you've previously believed won't get you where you need to go. Even right now you're looking for a fix, the right words, to get things back to normal with Lindsey."

He gets up and leaves the captain's seat, walking over close to me. He says the next sentence slowly and intensely.

"And your version of normal is exactly what is forcing your wife to contemplate a life without you. Am I making sense?"

I sigh. "Keep going. It's just that right now I'm fighting the clock."

"Still don't trust the old sea captain, huh? Still think you've got it figured out. You just need a few one-liners, and you're on your way. Steven, that's like bin Laden thinking he just needs a round of golf with the Dalai Lama. Then he can come out of hiding and start touring alongside Up with People."

I gesture out to the seawall. "You're aware no one's steering the boat, right?"

Andy turns to take back the wheel...and then drops his hands.

"Hey, look at that. We're coasting toward those big rocks. Wow, crashing into that would be bad news for everyone concerned, don't you think?"

I look at the approaching jetty. "Andy, don't mess around. I get your point."

"Listen, I keep driving weird. I keep making those big looping circles, and I'm always wanting to get up from the captain seat and walk around. I don't know what's wrong with me. Why don't you take over? You've been on this boat plenty of times."

"Stop it, Andy. I have no idea how to steer the boat. I've never even watched them operate it. That's not my deal. Now sit down and drive the boat."

We are now no more than two hundred yards from the rocks, moving slowly but still directly toward them.

"Whoa," he calls out like a casual observer. "Those rocks are getting *close*. It seems to me that if I just showed you how to turn the wheel, you could get in the chair and get us out of this crisis. I'd take the wheel if I were you. You're the answer guy. You're the big-time executive. This is your boat."

Andy throws his hands up. "Suddenly I just don't seem to know what the heck I'm doing."

"Andy, knock it off!" I yell. "You're putting your job at risk. You're putting *us* at risk."

He looks back at me. "Am I now? 'Cause I would have thought you could solve this. You don't need anyone. Man, those rocks look sharp, don't they? I mean, imagine what they'd do to the side of this boat. I'll sure have some explaining to do."

I jump up from my seat. "Andy, you're an idiot! You're gonna destroy a boat to make a stupid point?"

I run to the chair, take the wheel, and spin it hard, trying to maneuver us away from the rocks. But it's too late to steer it away. I panic and turn the wheel back hard the other way.

Less than a hundred yards from the rocks, Andy walks up behind me and pulls the engine handles into reverse. The boat continues forward for a moment and then slowly groans backward.

Andy sits back down at the wheel as I retreat to my seat.

"Wow, would you look at that," he marvels. "I never knew what those handle things were for. That was a close one!"

He gently turns the boat gradually back into the calm waters toward the slips.

I'm breathing hard, clenching my fists and trying not to punch him. His ridiculous game has convinced me of my greatest fear: he's a complete maniac. Neither of us talks for more than a minute. He's back to making lazy loops in the harbor.

"You're a jerk," I say.

"Yeah, I don't know what I was thinking there."

"Knock it off, Andy! Knock it off!"

He turns toward me again and quietly but firmly says, "No, *you* knock it off, Steven. Do you have any idea what I was doing a moment ago?"

"You were making a stupid point with a stupid analogy. And you almost damaged a really expensive boat while doing it."

"Actually," Andy replies, "we were never in any danger. We had plenty of time to make the turn. You just didn't happen to know that. If you kept trying to steer your way out of it, we might have been in danger. But as we were heading toward those rocks no matter how hard you tried to steer, it was just too late."

"I don't want to listen to you anymore."

"Look, you could be the best dang captain in the entire free world, and you still would've hit those rocks. Because you thought your steering would make a difference."

I can't look at him right now. I won't.

"Steven, this is exactly what you've been doing since long before I met you. That's where your life is right now—about eleven feet from the rocks. The boat is traveling at a pretty good clip, and you're doing everything you can to make the turn. And you can't navigate it. You've finally reached a place where steering doesn't do squat. Sharp course corrections don't matter anymore. God has been trying to teach you that lesson for a long time, but you've been making so much noise panicking and floundering at the wheel that you can't hear Him. Even right at this moment you still just want to get home and fix things up. And this time it is not going to end well. Do you hear me? You're about to lose your wife, your daughter, and your career. And you're irritated at me for trying to get your attention. Give me a break."

It's quiet again.

Finally, I ask, "So what do I do?"

"I'm gonna pretend, for the sake of argument, that you really want an answer to what you're asking, Steven," he says. "Let someone protect you. I, me, the guy you're sitting in front of, I happen to know, from slamming into rocks ten years ago, where the reverse handles are on the boat. God can use me to get you out of this mess and into waters that are smooth like glass, like you've never been in before."

I finally look up at him. "So maybe I wasn't quite as ready as you thought twenty minutes ago?"

"I don't know. You tell me."

"Andy, I honestly don't know if I'm lying, bluffing, pretending, or telling the truth at the moment. Every time I think I'm in, I've just been kidding myself. But I think for the first time, in this moment, I'm convinced at least you know what to do with me."

"Yeah, sometimes I do. Honestly, I'm just giving it my best shot most of the time. But none of us fully know how to do this. I'm still a hack. Jesus knows exactly what to do for you," he says. "And He probably wouldn't make you feel so dumb for it either. I'm sorry about that. But sometimes you just need someone who'll listen to point you in His direction."

"Forgive me for trying to take back the wheel. Where were we?"

Andy pauses and takes a deep breath. "I'm trying to get to the motive behind the behavior. It's one of the things that separates us from the Pomeranian. That and the whole opposable thumb deal. I think God wants you to stop just confessing your anger and admit the shame that causes you to attempt to control your life with anger.

"When you tell Lindsey your game plan, when you admit that rage allows you to get control over everything around you, for the first time in a very long time, she will believe you."

"That's it?" I hang my head. "All I have to do is admit I'm a jerk?"

"That's right."

"But that's what I always do."

"Ah," he says. "But this time, you have your true self to offer her as well. And when you do that, that happens to be the safest place in the world for her—the place where her own husband can be won. By making it about an anger problem and leaving it there, you're free to justify your anger. You're convinced your anger wouldn't be there if people would—if Lindsey would—just get in line and shape up.

"But when you admit the anger is there because *you want*

*it to be*—when you confess that you use anger because you're afraid of not being in control—you're telling her you are no longer justified. You're winnable. She's waited for that all these years. She's lived with a terrorist who never plays fair. And she's learned how to survive, how to negotiate the temporary appearance of peace. But she hasn't trusted the terrorist for years.... So she hasn't received his love for years. And so both of you have pulled apart. And that's the name of that particular tune."

"Geez." I sigh deeply. "You think you can write some of that down for me?"

We've reached our slip. Andy navigates the boat into place. "We're close to being able to send you home. But first, while the door is open, I want to say something else." He steers carefully, not looking at me while he speaks. "Are you ready?"

"Sure."

"This may be very painful."

"You mean unlike the rest of today?"

"Your shame drove you to control your world," he says. "So you used your anger as the method. Bad enough. But not as bad as this next thought. Ready?"

"No."

"You thought you were controlling others, but it was *you* being controlled all the time. It was your own trap. You were drinking your own poison." He glances up to see if I'm still with him.

"See, if you just ask God to help you stop using anger to control people, you're back at square one. Another behavior to conquer. But hey, if you were to discover that you can't get yourself out, no matter how hard you try, well, then you would really need God. Now we're talking real *repentance*. Get the picture?"

I make an involuntary grunt. "Nothing I can do, huh?"

"Nope. But listen to this: repentance isn't doing something about your failure. Repentance is admitting you can't do anything about your failure. It's not just agreeing you've done something wrong; it's admitting you can't do what needs to be done *to make it right*. God waits and yearns for that moment with everything in Him."

"I guess He's been waiting a long time," I say.

"I believe so."

Now that we're safely in our slip, he turns off the engine and motions toward the dock.

"Well, it's time, Steven. You no longer need me. You need to be talking to Jesus and then Lindsey."

"So, what do I say? To Him, I mean."

Andy turns his hands out toward me. "Sorry. No can do. That's for you and Him. Just tell Him the truth. He's been bringing you to this moment for a long time. He's really good at interpreting mumbles and sighs."

I still feel so lost, so uncertain. "What do I say to Lindsey? She doesn't trust me as far as she can throw me."

"There I *can* help," he says. "First, she shouldn't trust you, no matter what you tell her. Not for quite a while, probably. She'll have to watch and see if your repentance is authentic.

"The heart can't be talked into trust. Though she may not trust that you have yet fully changed, she can believe that you mean the words you're saying. She may not trust that you can make anything change yet, but she can at least believe your sincerity. That's a big deal. For now, it's the only deal you have. She hasn't believed you in a long time. If you want to get your foot back in the front door, ask her if she's ready to hear from you. If she says no, believe her and wait as long as she needs. This alone will cause her to ask who you are and what you've done with her husband."

Andy smiles at me, and I can't help smiling back.

"Don't tell her you're sorry unless you're willing to specifically lay out the truth of what you've been doing all along. She knows you're sorry about the behaviors, but she has waited for years to hear you tell the truth about yourself. This could take a while. Don't rush it.

"Then, and only then, should you ask her forgiveness. She might refuse. She probably should. She's pretty disgusted. In this too you must allow her readiness to determine everything. Just because you feel ready to be forgiven doesn't mean she's ready to forgive. The worst thing you can do is demand something she's not ready for. All this making sense?"

I motion to my outfit. "I'm out in public in my slippers."

"Tell her the truth of what you're discovering about yourself, about the secrets behind your actions. Tell her your fears. Tell her that you've poured your heart out to God and that you realize you need Him desperately for anything to change. Tell her that you can see you've been out of control and that you have no idea how to fix any of this. Tell her all that."

"Andy, don't you think it'll just frighten her more to hear that her husband is so out of control?"

"You think that'll be news to her?" He gently slaps my shoulder. "That doesn't frighten her. What frightens her is that you've never told her you realized it. She's had to watch you lie to yourself for so long. This will be the first time she's seen you in your right mind for a very long while. For the first time, she'll feel safety in knowing her husband is no longer the angry emperor with no clothes on."

"I'm, like, the worst husband in LA County."

"No. Not the worst." A smile turns at a corner of his mouth. "There are at least four others. Three of them are in prison. But the other guy's out on the street, holding a job."

I laugh out loud.

"And after you do all that," Andy says, "it would be great to tell her about my commitment to you. Tell her about our times together. Tell her about Bo's and the people you've met there. Tell her about your time at the Marriott. And Fenton's. Let her in on the whole process that has brought you to this moment."

I look up at him. "That may be harder to explain than the first part."

"Tell her you're beginning to discover how much you've hurt her over the years because you haven't trusted her with *you*. Tell her she is worthy of your trust and that you're ready to learn how to trust. Invite her into the process. Tell her you can't do it without her anymore. She may think you're reading lines off a cue card at first. This is not a game plan for an evening speech, but for the rest of your life."

Andy puts his hand on my arm.

"So, Steven, am I just putting words into your mouth, or are you ready to trust your wife with you?"

After a moment I nod. "Maybe for the first time in my life, Andy."

"Then get out of my hair," he yells. "I've got boats to log out. We'll meet up again when you're ready. Just write to me. Let me know when you're ready."

As I walk away, I turn back to Andy. "I think I'm supposed to say thank you. But I think I'll save it for later and see how this all goes first, if you don't mind."

"Fair enough. God bless you, Steven."

"Um, He's one of the two I'm not sure want to hear much from me right now. I wouldn't demand a blessing out of Him at the moment."

"Fair enough. Then God *endure* you. Better?" He smiles.

"Sounds about right," I say, nodding my head good-bye.

"I'll see you soon, Andy."

# "Go Figure. Andy Was Right."

*(Friday Afternoon, May 8)*

About an hour ago I left the marina and started driving. I found myself on the Pacific Coast Highway, heading north. I just had to drive to clear my head. I reached Malibu and have now turned around toward home.

No radio, no phone. Just the silence inside my Mercedes.

My mind wanders in my self-disgust. Ten miles maybe... past Las Flores, I begin to speak.

"I guess I thought I was supposed to figure it out, just manage it, and somehow life would work. I've always been smarter than everyone. So, then, how can someone with my intelligence rip apart his own marriage, be disdained at work, and feel so miserable? Andy tells me You've been waiting for me to ask that."

More miles. My mind drifts to disjointed snippets of growing up: childhood, my first girlfriend, sitting on the hood of my Mustang, in college with Ronnie Oliveri, getting drunk on Spanada, my first job after college, my wedding day... all the way to the tense, calculated, angry man sitting in Fenton's. It's like my mind is combing through old files, trying to figure something out....

"About a month ago I said it seems like something is whispering to me. It's the same whisper that's been there all my life. I've hidden from it, but it's always been there.

"It's always been You, huh?"

More miles. Past the Will Rogers State Beach turnoff.

"I want You to hear that I now know I've been blaming You and just about everyone else. I use my anger as my weapon of choice—to get my way, to control my world and leverage my positions. I've done it so long I don't know another way."

More miles.

"A big part of me doesn't want to face any of this. I want to drive, as fast as I can, somewhere I can hide, where I don't have to face what I've done, who I've been."

I speed past the turnoff for Pacific Palisades.

"No. I'm done running. It's time to face whatever You want me to face."

I am now entering Santa Monica. This place has my full attention. Coasting down this palm tree–lined boulevard here on the Pacific Coast Highway, all my senses are heightened. This is the scene of my successes, where I've made a name for myself. I'm always on my game here. I am known at these restaurants. I'm respected, given preference.

Sitting at the long stoplight at Wilshire, I take it all in. After the morning I've had, it all seems surreal: hollow, thin. Standing outside the crowded restaurants and bistros, everything seems so different now. Several years from now a whole new stable of thirty-four-year-olds will be given these window-side tables.

I park on Palisades Beach Road at the grassy strip of City Park that overlooks the Santa Monica pier. In my paint outfit I blend right in with the street people sharing cigarettes and scraps of lunch. Anytime now, well-dressed colleagues will start filling the ocean-view patios across the street, brokering at white-linen-covered tables procured earlier in the day by eager interns. I should be among them, bluffing my way through another day.

Instead I wander down to a secluded spot at a railing on a walking trail below me. I'm now facing the ocean and the landmark Ferris wheel on the pier's boardwalk below.

"Andy says that in all my controlling, I'm the only one who's really been deceived. The thought sickens me. Drains me. I want to make some sort of penance. But I guess that's part of the problem; I can't make up for any of it with more religious pretending. Please just forgive me for all my lying and pretending, the hurt I've caused. I can't stand how it feels like I've been wasting my life—and others'."

I stop talking as a couple strolls by on the path behind me. I turn and wait until they've passed.

"Andy also says I should trust You with the stuff I've never talked about. I don't really know how to do that. And I guess I always figured you were put-out, disgusted with me. You take care of the big stuff, but maybe You're here in the small stuff too. I want to believe that. I think that's the only way I'll get through this."

I take a deep breath, preparing for the next words. Somehow, I've been waiting to get to the place where I could say this my whole life.

"I'm sorry about who I've made You into all these years. Right now, I want You to take the real me—if You're really willing—all my fear and junk. I just give that to You. I don't want it anymore."

I want to say more, but...I think He understands what I'm trying to get out.

I don't want to leave this spot. This is the best I've felt since...I can't remember. But I have to see Lindsey. I climb slowly back up from the railing, walk across the park and to my car. I stand and stare across the street to the now-filled restaurant patios. Santa Monica is slowly being repainted with something real. As I walk to my car, I notice a street guy with oily, matted hair sitting on a bench, wearing socks on his hands. I find myself saying hello to him. I put the Mercedes in gear and slowly pull away from the curb and down the coast toward home.

Carlos said I'm a saint on my worst day. That I'm righteous right now. Me. Today, I think, is the very first time I've started to try that on. What if I'm really not defined by anything else? Steven, who can behave like a jerk... is a saint. Geez!

I don't want to manage the consequences anymore. I've done that all my life. Now I can't and I won't. Or I'll end up managing nothing.

As I work my way out of Santa Monica, I'm terrified of what I will face at the end of this drive home. But I can't control that. I can only trust Him with me.

I smile to myself, surprised that I'm actually beginning to believe what I just thought. What an incredible feeling.

Just this side of Manhattan Beach I say, *"I am asking with everything in me that You will do one thing: allow Lindsey to hear something she can start to believe. Beyond that, I don't even know what to ask. You take care of it."*

I feel like a man intentionally driving to his own execution. Ten thousand thoughts are now competing for my attention.

I'm not so much afraid that she'll be angry; for the first time, it actually matters more that she might not forgive me. Or that she'll let me in again, but for the same old wrong reasons. In the past I didn't care. I just wanted life back to normal. Now I don't know what I'll do if she lets me in again out of resigned fear.

*Just let her be there.*

I turn the corner into our cul-de-sac. Lindsey's car is in the driveway. Everything is moving in slow motion now. It seems like everyone I see has been brought up to speed on our situation. Melanie Patton is out watering some bushes, clearly positioning herself for my return. Her eyes follow my car with a disdainful glare that says, *"I've never trusted you from the day I first saw you. If I were her, I'd so dump you."*

I pull up in front of our house and turn off the engine. I sit there for a moment.

*Don't let me screw this up,* I silently plead.

Then I'm in our house. It's so quiet. Lindsey is not in the kitchen or the living room. I walk upstairs, past the bathroom and our bedroom. The last room at the end of the hall is Jennifer's. I walk up to the doorway. Lindsey is there, folding clothes on the bed.

"Hello," I call out tentatively.

She turns and looks at me. I hate that I have caused that look. It is a fragile but determined self-protection. She has had time to prepare a speech I'm hoping she won't have to give.

I blurt out, far too quickly, "Lindsey, I have so much I want to say to you."

She has turned away, folding more clothes.

"But you tell me when you're ready to hear it."

Nothing. As I turn to leave the room she says quietly, "Steven, I'm not ready to talk. I need to be alone."

It comes out in a guarded tone that confirms my fear that any trust we may have had is irretrievably gone. *Take my fear, God.*

I pause for a moment, deciding if I should say something more. I walk out of the room and down the stairs. I move slowly, hoping she'll call after me when she realizes I've actually honored her request to be alone. But there is nothing. I walk out the door and out to the sidewalk, past our cul-de-sac. When I finally stop, I'm in the middle of Crescent Park, nearly a mile away. I sit on a bench, feeling incredibly shaken. I'm afraid if I give Lindsey too long, she could give herself permission to leave me. But not too long later another thought presents itself.

Suddenly I realize something. *I've never done that before. I've never let her alone when she asked me to. And I didn't do it to gain an advantage. I did it because I want what she wants and nothing more. I love her but I'm not going to try to control her with that. Go figure. Andy was right.*

It's early evening by the time I get up from the bench and head home. I enter the house to find her at the kitchen sink, preparing dinner. I begin to climb the stairs but her voice stops me.

"You really look bad."

I stop and look down.

"I've been over most of Southern California like this."

We both stand motionless, neither of us sure what to say next.

"My sister told me I should divorce you."

"She's probably been talking to Melanie Patton."

She partially turns to face me, her hands still in the sink. "Are you just going to stand there?"

"I was going to go get cleaned up."

More silence.

"Help me set the table?" she asks. "After you're done?"

I nod, walk upstairs, and change my clothes. When I come back down, I enter the kitchen and wordlessly go about setting out three plates, three glasses, and three sets of silverware. For the next few minutes, a frightened couple finds whatever small comfort there is to be had in the routine of preparing dinner. Finally, Lindsey sits down at the far end of the table, facing away from me.

"I'm afraid, Steven."

"I know."

"I don't know what to do."

"I'm afraid too, Lindsey. But I'm trying to let God have that."

"How many times have we been here before?"

"Too many. Where's Jennifer?" I say, without looking up from folding napkins.

"I let her stay over at Kati's until dinner is ready." She taps a piece of silverware on a plate and says, "I can't do this anymore. I won't do this anymore, Steven. It can't keep being like this. This all has to change or... or— I don't know... what I'll do."

I long to jump in and tell her all that has happened to me in the last few hours. But this is what I always do, try to fix something, control things, cut off what she's trying to say. So I just stand there, shuffling plates around, nodding my head.

She asks, "Where had you been, dressed like that? You can't have gone to work."

"I've been with Andy, and then I drove for a while."

"So what did he tell you?"

"Lindsey, I don't even know where to start. I've been doing a lot of thinking."

"Like what?"

"Good stuff, I think."

She raises her head, our first real eye contact since morning. "Go ahead."

I take a deep breath. "Every time I've come home like this, after one of our fights, it's been to buy you off with an apology for my behavior. You know? But I'm not sure I've ever believed it was my problem. I told myself that you just got me upset with your irrational response. It would make anyone angry."

She turns toward me. "Is this the new good stuff? Because I gotta tell you—"

I gesture for her to be patient.

"So each time I would apologize for my behavior and promise not to get angry again. How many flowers? How many gifts to buy you back? But nothing ever changed."

She looks down at her hands. "It's gotten worse. Much worse, Steven."

"I know. Because I thought it was almost all about you. I'd think, *Yeah, maybe I get angry, but I'm right on almost everything else. Everybody else is screwed up, and I take the hit because I let my temper flare.* And I've been convinced I was right."

She looks up at me, waiting. "And so . . . ?"

"And so . . ." I pause for a moment. "I was wrong. None of that's true. *None* of it. It's a lie I told myself."

"What are you saying?"

"Let me try to get this all out, okay? I've got like four days' worth of stuff I want to tell you."

She leans back in her chair.

"Lindsey, I've used anger as a weapon to gain control. With you, at my job, even with Jennifer. I get angry to get my way. I actually thought it was working. Then one day I did it to you again, but I realized it was just for show. I saw that you were right, but I couldn't face it. I was devastated. I realized I'd been lying to myself and you for years. But I couldn't admit it to you. I was afraid of what would happen. I couldn't have explained it well then, and that's when I started driving around after work. I didn't know what else to do. I just knew I didn't want to be me anymore."

Lindsey says, "That night . . . when you called and told me not to hold dinner—that first time. I was so afraid I was losing you. I didn't know what to do."

I can see the pain in her eyes. Pain I've ignored a long time.

"Then I met Andy. He put up with me long enough for me to be able to face it—face my shame."

I look into her eyes, hoping she can sense my sincerity.

"The hardest thing he's said to me is this: while I'm trying to control others with my anger, my shame is controlling *me*. And you've borne the brunt of that for so long. You are married to a really unhealthy man.

"There." I raise my hands over my head like a soldier surrendering in battle. "Is that like the craziest thing ever? Hearing me talk like this?"

There's hesitation in Lindsey's voice. "I've waited a long time to hear you say something like this. And now that I'm hearing it, I don't know what to do. Am I supposed to say, 'All right, then,' and just go back to life like nothing ever happened?"

"No. You've done that too many times."

"I don't know what you're doing, or why you're saying this. I don't want to go through this again, Steven." Tears are forming in Lindsey's eyes. "I can't. I don't know if I can believe anything you say anymore."

"I know." I want to reach for her hands. "See, that's right, Lindsey. That's good. I don't know if you *should* believe anything I say. Just because I have some revelation at a marina doesn't undo a decade of manipulation."

"That's right, it doesn't."

She suddenly stands up, spins around, and angrily points her finger at me.

"No! Don't do this, Steven! This isn't fair. Don't play me! Don't do this!"

"I—"

"Shut up!" she yells. "I'd made up my mind. I had answers to all the justifications I knew you'd give. Then you pull this crap! Where was this three years ago? Huh? Don't do this. I can't do this anymore."

She's up and pacing around the kitchen, waving her arms and slamming pots on the stove. Tears are streaming down her face.

"What am I supposed to do?" she screams, running back to the table. "Tell me! What am I supposed to do with all this—this pain?"

"I'm sorry. I don't know."

She rushes up to me and yells, "Okay! You win. That's it. You win. You've worn me down. And this game of rehearsed lines you're playing with my head—I don't trust a damned word you're saying! Do you hear me? *I don't trust you!!!*"

I want so much to just grab her and hold her. But she isn't done. She shouldn't be done. All I can say is, "You're right."

She jerks away and moves to the kitchen counter, turns away from me.

"I'm ready to leave you, Steven. I *will* leave you."

"I know."

"What do you mean, you know?" She is sobbing and yelling now. "You *don't* know. You haven't known since we got married! If this is today's version of more flowers, just save it. I'm too tired. It's too late. I'm done."

She is now darting from one side of the kitchen to the other, putting something in the oven, slamming the oven door. She continues, still whirling and not looking.

"If you think nice words someone taught you to say are going to patch this up, you're stupider than I thought. Don't play me for an idiot. Don't do this, Steven!"

I'm sitting at the table. "Do you want me to go upstairs or something for a while?"

She spins around and yells, "Stop that! Stop playing the quiet, compliant husband! Do you know what I want? Do you?"

"Tell me," I answer quietly.

"I want you to tell me the truth. I don't need someone's counseling lines. I need you to tell me what's going on. Steven, do you not remember this morning? It was absolute insanity. Do you know Jennifer is totally freaked out? She's been texting me all day from school. What am I supposed to say to her? She's going to be home in a few minutes. What am I going to say to her? Tell me!"

I get up from my chair. "Okay," I say gently but more firmly. "Stop, all right? Will you listen for a second?"

She crumples back into her chair at the table, sobbing into her hands. "What am I supposed to do, Steven? Please, help me. . . ."

She puts her head on the table, sobbing almost uncontrollably.

I walk closer to her, but still at a distance. "I have no idea what to do. I've never felt more confused in my entire life," I say.

No response. Just sobbing.

"Lindsey, I know this all sounds like rehearsed crap. Even as I say it, I know it sounds that way. But I'm praying you know it's not. You don't have to say anything. Just listen. And when I'm done, you can call me a liar and ask me to leave. And I promise I will."

No response.

"I never trusted you with me—the real me. You or God. I didn't think you were trustworthy—I don't know why—so I kept you at a distance to protect myself. I used anger to push you and everyone else away. And maybe even more hurtful than my anger was how I didn't allow you to see me or really love me. You've had all this love to give, all this you've wanted to say to me, and I made you pay for it when you tried. What can I say? I can't make it up to you. I can only tell you that I'm here now. And I'm so desperately sorry, not because

I want things to go back to normal, as if they ever were, but just that this time I want you to know you were right. I know I've destroyed your heart. I know that much. And I just want to beg your forgiveness. Not just for the things I've said or for breaking your heart so many times, but for trying to control you with my anger all these years. Lin, now that I see it I'm so sorry for what I've put you through.... You don't have to forgive me. You shouldn't. But I sure want it if you think you ever can."

I touch the top of the table next to her.

"I've caused you to question who you are. I've beaten your dreams out of you. I'm not expecting or asking you to trust me. *I* don't trust me—I'm like a scared little kid lashing out at anyone who gets in my way. Just try to believe this: I am truly, unbelievably sorry. I've repented before God the best I know how. And I asked Him for the first time to do what I was never able to do."

Lindsey sits up slowly and looks at me. Her face is a red and puffy mess, covered in wet hair and tears.

"Lindsey, I'm getting this all garbled. A bunch of this is what Andy's pointed out and I'm saying it really poorly. I'm only trying to understand it and make the words mine. Whatever you do next, I just needed you to hear me say this."

She sniffles. "You're not saying it poorly."

"Lindsey." I want to grab her hands so badly, but I don't. I won't. "If it's going to change, it has to start with me. I think God sent Andy. I think He wants to show me how to dismantle this twisted character I've created. These are Andy's thoughts, but they're the best things I've heard for years—maybe ever. I need to start believing who God says I am and live from that. I'm not a screw up. I'm not hopeless. That's what I'm trying to believe. That's my whole game plan. If I can't start to believe that, then...you *should* leave me."

She shakes her head and looks down at the table, wiping at her eyes.

"I'm so confused, Steven. Is this you, or what Andy wants you to believe?"

I smile. "You know me, Lin. I wouldn't have seen this on my own. I think that's why Andy's here. For the first time in a long time, I'm hopeful that I can believe this. So I guess it's both Andy and me. His thoughts, God's thoughts, or mine, this is what I need to believe."

I smile a little and take a step closer to her, still giving her room.

"I need you. You see me better than anyone. You can tell me the truth. I want you to tell me when you see me going toward anger, toward protecting myself, when I'm getting scared or lashing out or whatever I do. You can hold me to it. I want you to, and if I don't let you, you shouldn't trust me and I should go."

"You really want me to tell you that? How do I know you'll let me?" she asks.

"I'm sure I won't always respond well. I'm not used to this. But tell me what you're doing and I'll try to remember and let you help me."

"You're serious."

"As serious as I get. And even if you do it badly, I'll work hard to listen to you. You telling me what you see is a hundred times better than me trying to figure it out in the heat of the moment. It won't be easy, but you can test me on this and see if I mean it."

She is turned away again, thinking it through, I suppose.

I kneel down by her chair. "Will you look at me?" She does. "This isn't another attempt to buy a get-out-of-the-doghouse-free card. You believe me?"

Lindsey looks down for a moment. Then she straightens

up and looks deeply into my eyes for a long time. We're only a couple of feet apart.

"I believe you," she says. "I don't know what it means, but I do believe you're sincere. I can't help but think it will only last a few days, until the next blowup. But I want to help if you think I can."

"Thank you."

She looks into my eyes. "I've let you back in so many times before. I always hoped you'd change, but I never really believed you would. Mostly, I was terrified of losing everything if I didn't. In spite of everything, I do love you. And I always wanted your apologies to be real. I just didn't want our life together to be over. How messed up is that? I don't think I've *ever* believed you. And I don't think things are really going to change even now."

"That's not messed up. That's rational. You were just scared. You didn't know what else to do."

She pauses and looks at her hands, clasped together in her lap. "I choose to forgive you today though, and not because I'm afraid to leave. If this is a game, I'll be gone. But I think you're telling me the truth, for the first time in a very long while. I want to see if you'll let me really help you, whatever that means. I still want to be... to be with you." She looks up at me. "Do you realize how long I've hoped for that? No. You can't. You cannot possibly understand—"

Her voice breaks off, and she begins weeping again. But this weeping is different. She leans in toward me. I desperately want to hold her. Still, I wait for a moment, not wanting to frighten her. But she stays pressed against me. So I take her into my arms.

And I hold her as tenderly as I've ever held anything in my life.

# "Where Do We Go from Here?"

*(Monday Evening, May 11)*

The weekend is filled with long walks around the neighborhood. Slowly, Lindsey and I start to talk our way through things that have been ignored for a long time. Sometimes the conversation starts to get heated, but I find myself immediately backing off and letting things cool down. I'm starting to learn to admit it a little quicker when she lets me know my anger is ramping up.

I take Monday off, which surprises Lindsey. We drive up the coast to a tiny café in Carpinteria that we used to visit a lot when we were first married. In the same corner booth where we celebrated our first anniversary, we linger over some great food and wine. The place is nearly empty. I tell her the story of meeting Andy and my first trip to Bo's. About Cynthia, Carlos, Hank, and Bo himself. We are still awkward and tentative. But as I get to talking about the deck crowd's humor, we start to relax and laugh together.

Later in the evening, we are leaning back, together, in the same side of the booth, finishing off our biscotti and Italian coffees. We're happy being quiet together. Eventually Lindsey asks me, "So, where do we go from here?"

Something beautiful and fragile has happened. But we both agree we don't know how to turn this around by ourselves. Reaffirming our love and commitment to each other won't do it alone. There's still so much we're unwilling to touch. We're both afraid we'll soon figure out how to undo the magic God worked for us several days ago.

All of a sudden, I suggest something that would have sounded ridiculous even yesterday. I ask her to accompany me to Bo's.

"Lindsey," I say, "we've got to go there." I find myself repeating Andy: "They have a shrimp cocktail that'll cure rickets. They serve it on a plate. *On a plate,* for crying out loud!"

She laughs at me. "Do you think they'd mind? It is *your* place."

"Once they get some time with you, I won't be invited anymore."

"I would like to meet Andy."

"I'd like that too." I squeeze her hand tightly in mine.

"I'll send him an e-mail. He can pick us up. He'd love that. You just gotta take a ride in his car. We don't happen to have any out-of-style sunglasses lying around, do we?"

"I don't know. Why?"

"You might need 'em. Never mind. I'm sure he's got plenty. You're gonna love the Electra. Just wait."

"But didn't you tell me that he sold the Electra?" she asks.

"Yes, he did," I answer. "Yes, he did."

It's eleven thirty the next morning. And I'm walking up the stairs to the patio deck at Bo's. I've come by myself, having called ahead and learned Andy would not be here until after noon. Perfect. As I reach the deck I spot Cynthia, Carlos, and Hank, all sitting together at their regular table. I'm incredibly nervous. Each of them, as well as others from tables nearby, call out my name. I am silent as I stand in front of them.

Carlos says, "Dude, you gonna say something?" Then,

"Oh, I get it—we're playing charades!" He excitedly rubs his hands together. "Give me a second. I love this game! Two words? Is it like the name of a movie? Come on, man, give us something. I can't do this alone."

I love Carlos.

I am not sure what to do next. Everything I rehearsed on the drive over seems corny now. So instead, I reach into my pocket and pull out a single key and place it on the table in front of Hank.

"What's this?" he asks.

I pause before I can answer.

"It's the key to Andy's Electra."

The deck area near the table goes silent. Everyone is staring at the key.

"But...how...?" Hank mutters, unable to finish his sentence.

"It's a long story," I answer, repeating Hank's line from our last time together. He looks up at me for a long time. Then, slowly, his face forms a deep, warm smile. He nods his head. I smile back at him, and nod mine. I turn to see Cynthia and Carlos grinning like proud parents. Sometimes things actually work out better than you can rehearse them. This is one of those times.

"Hank, if you would, tell Andy the paperwork's in the dash. The car's all his."

He looks at me and then over to Carlos. He shakes his head, looks back at me, and smiles. "I'd be glad to, Steven."

I turn to walk away. After a few steps I turn and come back.

I look directly into Hank's eyes. "Thank you, Hank. It was your care for Andy that got his car back. It was your care for me that made me go get it."

He pushes his chair back, stands up, and reaches for my

hand. He shakes it firmly and slowly. "No, you're wrong, Steven. This was all you, my friend. This was all you."

I wave to everyone and then turn to walk away. I don't want to spoil this moment by saying something stupid. As I reach the stairs I look back. Hank is still standing there, holding the key in his hand.

## "How Have I Missed This Kind of Life?"

*(Noon, Thursday, May 14)*

The headlights and grille of Andy's Electra seem to follow me through the parking lot, smiling gratefully, as I walk to my car. Freshly waxed and meticulously shined up, the owner agreed to bring Andy's car to Bo's before noon in the same condition he bought it. At the price he charged me, it's the very least he could do. The guy didn't really want to sell the car. He said he'd been looking for one like that for as long as he could remember. That's never a particularly good situation for the buyer.

I still can't believe I was able to track it down. I called a friend with software to locate recent property sales and used-car transactions. But the retitling must have not fully gone through yet. He couldn't find a thing for a 1970 Electra in all Southern California. Then it dawned on me that I could check out Web sites of Electra owners. It's crazy. There must be two dozen sites! For a car that hasn't been produced since I was a boy. After combing through discussions about tail fin heights in various years and the comparative merits of particular muffler housings, I finally stumble upon it. A guy's bragging about locating and purchasing the car of his dreams.

"This baby is incredible! A pristine 1970 Buick Electra. She's a cherry-apple red convertible. A convertible! What are the chances of stumbling onto one of those? You *never* see 'em anymore. Killer! And to top it off, a previous owner installed front-seat tuck-'n'-roll upholstery from a car of Cary Grant's. *Cary freaking Grant!*"

I knew I had found Andy's car.... I also knew it was probably gonna cost me more than my Mercedes to get it back. And I didn't care. I was so excited to find it.

As I drive back up the coast, I am filled with this incredible sense of satisfaction. I don't think I can remember ever doing anything like this—in maybe my entire life.

*Where have I been? How have I missed this kind of life?*

Andy taught me this. He's been waiting for me to learn it so I could pass it on. I'm sure he never thought it would come back around to him like this. Go figure.

It is a phenomenal drive back to work. I can't stop smiling.

It's time to take Andy up on his offer to get back together. I decide so say nothing about the car. I'm dying to. But I don't want to mess things up. I'll wait until he says something. The essence of our e-mail interaction went like this:

> Andy,
>
> Hello, friend. So much to talk to you about. When we were last together you asked me to write once I was ready to have you come pick me up. I think I'm ready. Except I'd like my wife to come along, if you don't mind.
>
> Sincerely,
> Steven

> Steven,
>
> Well, well, well... So Lindsey wants a ride in the old Buick, eh? I tell you, the ladies love the old Electras.

Hard to explain. They're not as sexy as your GTOs or Barracudas. But something about that cushiony drive shaft just seems to hit 'em where they live.

So, Thursday at 11:00 a.m.?

Andy

Just honk, and we'll come right out. Thanks for everything, Andy.

Steven

So, just wondering. Is this the thanks you were gonna wait on until you saw how things went?

Andy

Yeah, I think it's that thanks.

Steven

Then, you're welcome.

Andy

*And just when I'm thinking that's it—that he's not going to mention the car:*

Hey, Steven . . . ?

Yes?

Thank you, my friend. I'm not sure what to say. Thank you. . . .

Andy

# "So the Suit Found a Date, Huh? What the Deal Is with Dat?"

*(Late Morning, Thursday, May 21)*

He should be at our house any minute. I'm more anxious right now than when Andy showed up at my office. We're about to sail into uncharted waters. What if Lindsey doesn't like him right away? *I* sure didn't. What if she's put off by the crowd at Bo's? What if she doesn't get their humor? What if they don't get her?

Lindsey shyly walks down the stairs. She is wearing a pair of sunglasses with oversize frames.

I smile up at her. "Where did you find those?"

"Chanel. They're retro. They're actually pretty stylish."

"Well, thanks. They should make Andy very happy."

Then comes the sound of a horn.

We open the door to see Andy standing behind the Electra's fully opened passenger door. He is wearing baggy shorts, flip-flops, sunglasses, the ever-present L.A. Dodgers hat, and one of the three or four Hawaiian shirts I've ever seen him in since I met him. The dark blue one with the hula girls. Geez.

Lindsey has been unusually quiet all morning, so I take charge. "Andy, this is my wife, Lindsey. I've told her all about you. Or, as much as I thought she could bear."

Andy totally ignores me, smiles at Lindsey, and reaches

for her hand. "I'm really glad to meet you, lovely lady," he says, with just the slightest bow.

"May I say," he adds, referring to her sundress, "yellow is definitely your color."

I give him a look. *Don't push it, old-timer.*

Lindsey breaks into a beautiful smile at Andy's greeting. She looks great, even in those ridiculous glasses.

And then, suddenly, she throws her arms around Andy and gives him a very tender hug.

Have you ever had one of those moments that freezes time and seems to last for minutes? This is one of those. My mind flashes to that night at Fenton's when Andy promised me his car could take us to the places I needed to go. And now, here in my front yard, my wife, full of gratitude and hope, is hugging this unlikely driver who has brought me to those places.

"Now, those…*those* are sunglasses. See, Steven? Didn't I tell you? It's not just a thing from my generation. Classy young, hip women get it."

I don't have the heart to tell him….

As he ushers us both into the backseat he mumbles under his breath, but loud enough for us both to hear, "It never ceases to amaze me how one can have such great taste and the other so little. The guy must be a great kisser. That's all I can say."

Then we're off. He was right. Lindsey loves the car. And she appears completely delighted and comfortable with Andy. It's a beautiful, clear day, and she's beaming as he brings the car up to speed on the Coast Highway from Manhattan Beach toward Bo's.

I look over at my wife. Her beautiful dark brown hair is blowing behind her. Her eyes are closed, drinking in the cool, morning wind. She scrunches closer to me and puts her arm in mine.

For the first time in a very long time, I am actually *in* the moment, fully enjoying it, fully a part of it. For so long I was watching my life from a distance, critiquing everyone and everything in it. Standing outside its enjoyment. Today it's as if that whole way of coping has blown out the top of Andy's convertible.

Before too long I sit up and realize we're driving down Washington Boulevard—that ribbon of asphalt forming well back into Los Angeles proper and eventually dwindling to a single congested lane, dividing Venice from Marina del Rey. It ends in a cul-de-sac a few steps from the boardwalk and from Bo's.

The anxiousness returns.

How will my hygienically sensitive wife respond when Hank and Carlos take food from her plate? Will Bo swear at her?

Bo greets us as we walk through the louvered front doors of Pacific Bayou.

"So the suit found a date, huh? What the deal is with dat?"

"Bo," Andy intervenes. "This is Steven's wife, Lindsey."

She brightens. "Steven has told me about you, Mr. Bo."

"*Mr.* Bo?" He thinks for a moment, tilting his head. "Hmm. I like dat. I'm likin' dat a lot!"

He yells into the restaurant, to the staff at the front desk, several yards away: "You hearin' that in there? This beautiful woman, she calls me *Mr.* Bo! Time da rest of you be showin' that kind of respect! Startin' today, it's Mr. Bo around here.

"Mr. Bo." He rears back and laughs out loud. "I does like the sound of dat."

He spins back around to my wife.

"You eatin' free today, pretty lady. Suit, he'll be payin' double, but *you*, you're eatin' free!"

We're ushered through the restaurant and up and outside onto the deck. I've missed just hanging out here. Hank and Carlos are sitting at the same table in the middle of the deck, like they haven't gotten up since the very first time I visited. I think Hank's even wearing the same shirt.

Pulling out a chair for Lindsey, Andy, acting like a maître d', says, "Sit right here, young lady. I called ahead and told them you two were coming. Bo wanted us all at the special table today."

Bo politely hands Lindsey a menu and then barks at the rest of us. "Okay, here the deal is: We're outta most everything on the menu. You got boiled carp and scary mussels left over from last Sunday. You get you one check, not all separate. That way maybe at least one of you be a decent tipper. Not a bunch of pocket change. Have you a nice day, an' don't make a mess!"

He turns to Lindsey and says under his breath, "You like shrimps?"

"Uhm... yes," she says.

"You lucky today, pretty lady," he says, snatching the menu back from her. "I take care of you."

As Bo turns to badger more of the deck crowd, I take a deep breath and say, "Lindsey, this is Carlos and this is Hank."

Stating the obvious, I add, "I—I've told you a lot about them."

Carlos and Hank jump up like a couple of seventh graders about to pull a prank.

Hank blurts out, "Hi, we're the Wasabi brothers. Everything you've heard about us is true."

Carlos steps directly in front of Hank and takes Lindsey's hand. "Please, let Carlos Badillo shelter you from my remedial friend. He's not so well. And don't feed him nothing.

You won't be able to get him off your lap. Welcome to Bo's, Lindsey. We're all really happy you're here."

Hank steps back next to Carlos. He says proudly, "We were a little rough on your husband a couple of times back. We weren't sure we'd ever see him back here." He forces an expression that almost rises to a smile.

Bo barges in with Cynthia on his arm, beaming as if he's just won a prize at the fair. Depositing her in a chair next to Hank, Bo leans in to Lindsey and says under his breath, "Dis lady you gotta know. She's the one keeps all these crawfish in line. They don't be skippin' out with a bad tip with her around. More customers like this lady, and maybe someday you gonna see Bo shut down this crab shack, move down the Trinidad way, and spend all day drinkin' rum and playin' Sudoku."

He laughs as if he's the funniest thing he's met all day. The deck crowd joins in.

Just behind them Keith, Cynthia's husband, walks in wearing a commercial pilot's uniform.

"Hey, everybody, look!" Carlos says, bowing deeply. "The flyboy returns from the Orient! With spices and... what... abacuses? Hey, man! Welcome home."

Everyone stands to greet him. Keith looks like what you'd hope the pilot on your flight would look like. Tall, professional, solid, and stable-appearing. His greetings are warm but precise. Standing next to Hank, I imagine a picture of them in the dictionary next to the word *contrast*.

Hank lights up. "You bring back any of those bags of honey-roasted peanuts?"

"Sorry, Hank. All they've got now is what they call 'pretzel medley.' "

Hank shakes his head.

"When did the pretzel get to medley status?" Carlos questions. "You gotta earn your way to medley status, man. *Fruit* medley—now *that's* a medley. Remember? You had your pears in there, man, grapes and peaches and maraschino cherries and who knows what else? The whole thing swimming around in, like, mango juice or something. *That's* a medley. What, you add some bland dough sticks to pretzels, and suddenly some marketing suit calls it a medley? I don't think so."

Andy looks off in the distance, wistful. "I'm so old I can remember when they gave you real silverware with the meals. In coach!"

"You got meals? When did *that* stop?" Hank bellows.

Keith sits down next to Cynthia. "About the same time they started making *plastic* pilot's wings for us to hand out to the kids."

I offer my hand to Keith.

"Hello. I'm Steven and this is my wife, Lindsey."

"I'm pleased to meet you both," Keith says as he shakes my hand. "I'm sorry it's taken so long for this introduction. I'm in the air three out of four Thursdays. So I miss out on a lot of deck action."

Keith hugs Cynthia tightly. "I've really missed you, my wife. How's the book coming? Are we going to be rich?"

"I'd keep your day job." They hug each other again.

Soon we are all sitting at the table. The banter is flowing freely, but Lindsey seems, to me, unusually subdued and quiet. Well, of course. These guys are a lot to handle the first time. She'll settle in and really enjoy this.

Cynthia makes an attempt to draw Lindsey into conversation a couple of times, but for some reason my wife—usually pretty social—isn't entering in.

*What's going on? Is she willfully trying to not like this? Maybe because I think this is a great place and because these are my friends, she's going to go silent and pretend to not enjoy herself? Is that what's happening here?*

"Lindsey," I whisper. "Is everything all right?"

"It's great. Really. I'm fine." That's all she gives me.

*Something's wrong. I can feel it. I've been here before. I know this feeling. Still . . .*

Cynthia smiles and places her hand on my arm but addresses Lindsey. "These guys are pretty random. I don't even try to keep up. I just let them babble."

*Cynthia must feel it too. She can see what Lindsey's doing. They all can.*

"What do you mean, babble?" Carlos objects. "My man Hank and I, we don't babble."

"Right." Cynthia rolls her eyes. She now places her hand on Lindsey's arm. "Just before you got here, they spent several minutes debating whether the boulders on the hills outside Temecula are actually giant petrified vegetables. I rest my case."

"That's important talk," Carlos defends. "This is how science got started. Guys like us."

A shrimp cocktail is placed in front of my wife. Lindsey looks at it and says, "Why is it on a plate? I thought you were joking about that."

*I can't believe she's saying this.*

"Come on, Lindsey," I plead. "It's cool. It's different. Just taste it."

There is an awkward silence at the table.

"Just try it," I say louder, fully embarrassed.

*I only said what everyone else was thinking. Geez, it's like nothing has changed. You try to do something a little more fun and unusual, and unless it comes from her, she can't get with it.*

"I wasn't complaining, Steven." She takes a bite. "It's good.

I thought you were kidding about it being on a plate, that's all. Then they bring it on a plate and...I didn't mean anything by it. I've just never seen shrimp cocktail on a plate."

Carlos pats her on the back. "It's great, huh? I love how they put all those purple onions around the shrimp. Keeps my people in jobs. Now that you've tasted it, you're gonna keep coming back. I know it."

*Oh, come on. Now she's got Carlos trying to make her feel better because she's got such an insensitive husband. Yeah, I'm such a bad guy. And by the way, Carlos, that's the same line you used on me the first time I was here. Come up with a new one sometime, huh?*

"So, Lindsey," Andy says suddenly. "Tell us about you. How long have you been putting up with this bozo?"

Lindsey looks at me and then quickly down when our eyes meet. "We met when I was a senior in high school."

"Oh," Carlos helps. "So you two go back a ways. That's great."

He's trying to help make things work, but my wife is giving absolutely nothing. She barely looks up.

Andy's staring out at the ocean. He seems slightly embarrassed. Maybe he's thinking this wasn't such a good idea. This is just what I feared. She doesn't get what goes on here.

A conversation full of easygoing banter has quickly become stilted and forced simply because my wife can't relax and enjoy something a little different from her regular day-to-day.

A server sets a crab salad in front of Cynthia.

Andy steps in. "I'm really glad you two were able to join us today."

I can tell he's trying to smooth things over. Lindsey's strangeness has got me completely off balance. I should just take her aside in private and tell her I'm frustrated, but that seems even more awkward.

"These are good people, Lindsey. They've become friends of mine."

Nothing more than a clumsy nod.

*It amazes me how my wife can get everybody rushing to her defense simply by playing the frightened, unhappy child. I've seen it so often, but never as clearly and blatantly as right now. All I wanted was for her to meet these people I've come to know and enjoy, and the very fact that I enjoy them is her signal to derail the day.*

"Lindsey, why don't you at least say something?" I ask. "People are talking to you, and you're giving them nothing."

"She seems to be eating shrimp," Hank says, giving me a furrowed brow.

*No, Hank, she's trying to wreck the day for me.*

I sigh and look down at my hands. "I'm sorry. I thought you'd enjoy this place."

She looks up at me with a hurt expression, trying to telegraph to the whole table what a bad person I am.

"What do you want, Steven? I *am* enjoying this place."

I can feel several pairs of eyes burning into me. "You know exactly what I'm talking about, Lindsey."

"What? What are you talking about? Steven, stop it. You're doing it again."

Her voice is loud and piercing.

*Great! Now you're mad. And you're going to let everyone see it. Now I've done something so terrible, and you're angry and so you're justified, right? You win. You put on a show, stack the deck. Yep, looks like you got what you wanted.*

"Steven, I don't think—" Cynthia starts, but I cut her off.

"What are you getting bent out of shape about, Lindsey? How hard is it for you to just enjoy yourself, enjoy this place? You're acting like it's this huge burden."

"A huge...?" She glares at me, and then her eyes turn to the others at the table.

*No you don't. Don't go after their sympathy. Stand up for yourself if you're so innocent. This is between you and me.*

"Steven, do you remember you asked me to tell you when you're doing it. Well, you're doing it."

"No, I'm not!"

"Please! Just stop it." The last part she hisses through her teeth.

The next few moments are a blur. I snap back with something, and Andy is suddenly trying to calm me down like I'm an out-of-control kid.

*No, Andy. That's not right. That's not what's going on here!*

And then I just blow. I say some really stupid, really mean things that all seem necessary in the moment. Suddenly Lindsey is on her feet, crying. She tries to get away, but discovers there is no exit in the direction she has run. Still crying, she's forced to turn around and walk past us all before she can get off the deck and down the stairs.

I stand to go after her, but I feel Hank tugging my arm and blocking my path.

I hear Cynthia say, "Hey, Steven, I'll go down and find her, okay? Why don't you just hold on a second, dear."

Everyone is trying to not stare at me. That's when it hits. The avalanche of realization. The crystal clarity of knowing what you've done a split second after it's irretrievably out there. I've hit the Send button, and the e-mail is gone. And I can't unsend it. In a matter of seconds I can see the entire conversation, the entire scene from three or four angles that simply did not cross my mind until this moment. I've lost it again.

I look around the deck. Everyone is frozen in their places. I am suddenly hit with an overwhelming wave of shame and embarrassment. I am angry, at myself. Angry that I could let myself get this exposed. Angry and afraid that I broke my promise.

Hank is still standing next to me. A moment ago he was blocking my path. Now I realize he has an arm around my shoulder.

"You okay?" he says, looking directly at me with incredible care and concern. For the first time I realize Hank is my ally.

"I blew it," is all I can say.

He gently turns me around and guides me back into my chair. Carlos is leaning in across the table. "You okay, man?" he asks quietly. "What's going on?"

*What is going on?* I have no idea. I have no explanation for what just happened. How did I not see what was happening and get a grip on it?

Hank has moved to Lindsey's chair. He picks up a shrimp from her abandoned plate and says, "Did you think you wouldn't mess up again? Because you will, you know."

"I do now."

I start up out of the chair. Andy, who is sitting on the other side of me, puts his hand on my shoulder and gently but firmly pulls me back down.

"I've got to go after her," I explain.

"I really want you to listen to me right now," Andy says strongly, getting up to stand in front of me. "She's had enough lunch for one day."

Cynthia surfaces at the stairs. "Hon, um, I can take Lindsey home. I'd be really glad if you'd let me do that for you. She's in my car right now."

I just nod my head.

"It's gonna be all right, Steven," Cynthia calls out to me. "These things take some time, don't they?" Then she is off down the stairs and out to her car, where my wife sits.

There is more quiet at the table.

"Well, looks like you're driving me home, Mr. Badillo," Keith says to Carlos.

Next thing I really remember, I'm sitting in the passenger seat of Andy's Electra, staring out over the ocean from our old spot up on the cliffs.

*Here I am again... again. I've done it. She'll never believe me again.*

Andy is working on his cigar and listening to some of the saddest music I think I've ever heard. We've been sitting here for at least ten jets passing over.

I finally speak. "I gotta tell you, this is hard. I know you're all here for me... for us... but it feels so horrible, like Lindsey and I are this loser couple that everyone feels sorry for. I'm not used to being pitied."

Andy strikes a match and places it to the end of his cigar, painstakingly lighting it completely before blowing out his match. Only then, after his first full puff of smoke, does he say, "What you mean is, you're not used to *knowing* that you're being pitied."

"Are you saying I've been pitied and haven't seen it?"

Andy nods. "Probably. Not only on the deck. Even people at work, where you think the whole place is against you. There are many there who could be good friends. You can't let that happen for fear that if you let them see your mess, they'd pity you. Tragedy is, they already do. You gain all the pity but none of the friendship. One thing for certain, they don't see your facade as strength or health."

"What am I going to do, Andy?"

"What are you going to do? Well, you could move... to the Baltic Sea. I don't think anyone there pities you, yet."

"I'm serious."

He puffs again on his cigar. "Well, let's take an inventory. What's changed since our talk at the marina?"

"Apparently nothing."

He makes the sound of a game-show buzzer. "Oh, I'm sorry. Wrong answer. But we do have some lovely parting gifts for you...."

"Andy, I mean it. I'm right back where I was last time. Actually, I'm worse off because now I've made the apology, made the promises, made the last-ditch statements about how I now realize the truth. And I still blew through all the barricades at the first opportunity. What can I say now that she'll listen to? What? That I *really, really* mean it this time?"

"Hold on," he says, his eyebrow creeping up. "Did you mean what you said the other day, or was that just a ploy? Because I thought for sure when you left me, that you were sincere."

"I really thought I was," I answer.

"Then you meant what you said? You told her the truth?"

"Yes."

"So, if you told her the truth and it wasn't a ploy, then why wouldn't you just tell her the truth again?"

It's at moments like these that I have to take a deep breath and remind myself that at some point Andy usually comes around to making sense.

I look over at him. "How many times can I tell her the truth and then *prove* to her it wasn't really true?"

"Your sincerity and desire *were* true; your insights were true; your love was true. Behaving today like a raving lunatic didn't change any of that."

I nod. Okay, he's starting to make sense.

"So I'm supposed to just go back and admit that I'm wrong again?"

"You got something else? Steven, listen to me. The truth is all you've got. You're not going to come up with something else or something better. This is where we happen to be. And you aren't going to miraculously transform from

Attila the Hun to Mr. Rogers in a heartbeat, just because you told her you wanted to. The truth is—in case you haven't noticed—you have a bit of a tendency to blow. And if you want to someday start to get past that tendency, there is really only one solution. You'll have to keep admitting it and let God and some humans who love you begin to protect you. That truth's all you got."

"But how many times is she going to put up with me messing up?"

"Well," he says, blowing out a huge plume of smoke, "I don't know. I don't know how far you've pushed this thing. I don't know how much you've torn her down. She may already be done. But I don't think so. If she believed what you said last week, and if she loves you as much as she appears to, then my answer is: probably as many times as it takes for you to stop acting this way. Hopefully you'll get there before she cracks. Here's my ace in the hole—for you *and* her: if you keep telling the truth, regardless of how embarrassing, it'll have a profound effect on *you*. It'll begin to free and heal you. And you'll begin to actually behave like less of a Neanderthal. I'm thinking she's bound to pick that up. So the gamble is whether she can hold out that long, whether she *should* hold out that long."

"So, I've got to go back and tell her the whole thing again?"

"Tell her why you lost it. Tell her what you were thinking, your whole process."

He inspects his cigar for a long time, spinning it in his fingers. "Do you know why you lost it?"

"I just...it really seemed, in the moment, like she was intentionally trying to not like Bo's."

Andy takes another long draw on his cigar. "Steven, are you ready to hear something hard again?"

"Do I have a choice?"

"No, not really."

"Then go ahead."

"Steven, do you know that the rest of us were truly enjoying your wife? Do you know that none of us found her to be anything but a really delightful person? Do you know that if it came to a vote, most would probably trade your place at the table for her?"

"You're kidding, right?"

"Do I look like I'm kidding?" he answers, with a no-nonsense stare.

"No."

Andy adjusts his ball cap. "Any chance this was entirely about you again? About you wanting all of us to be so deeply impressed by her so we'd all think *you* were more impressive? Any chance?"

I can't look him in the eye.

"Steven, I'm your fan—at the moment, perhaps your biggest fan. But this lunch never had a chance from the start. You were so full of unfair expectations of Lindsey. She never had the opportunity to be *herself,* only some image you've created her to be—an idealized person with just the right humor, intelligence, and debonair to impress your witty new friends. Such a person does not exist. Such a person is not nearly as impressive and delightful as the real Lindsey. It all gets created from that self-story of shame that says you, at all costs, must be admired, respected, in control. So you try to force everyone in your world into that mold. But people, not trapped in your self-story, they don't fit so easily into those molds. They're not even sure, from moment to moment, how you want them to perform."

"Don't hold back. Speak your mind," I say, trying to smile.

"And when she doesn't perform right, you judge her, thinking she's trying to sabotage you. This makes you even angrier, more irrational and more stupid. The saddest part is that Lindsey is trying so hard to be whoever she thinks you want her to be. But she can't figure out the rules. So she keeps disappointing you. And eventually, even those who love well have to leave the game. Because love has no home in such a game."

Andy lets me take in his speech, peering into the rearview mirror, removing something from the corner of one eye. Squinting at his index finger to discover what he just removed, he says, "Any chance I'm right about what I just said?"

After a long time fiddling with the glove compartment button, I say, "I think I'd better get home. I need to talk to my wife. If she'll let me."

The Electra starts up and ambles down the hill toward my home.

## "Why Do You Get So Angry?"

*(Thursday Evening, May 21)*

Andy drops me off at my house around two thirty. Nobody is home. So I drive to Santa Monica and work late. I leave a text, telling Lindsey I'll grab a bite to eat at the office. I don't try to say anything else. I walk inside our house sometime after ten. Again, there is a light flickering in the family room. Jennifer again is in the dark, watching television.

"Hey, kid."

"Hello, Dad." She doesn't look up at me.

"Mom up?"

"I don't think so."

"So, homework all done?"

She sighs and shakes her head. "Dad, do you realize that's the first thing you almost always ask me?"

"I do? Sorry. I'm guess it's just because I'm a dad. That's what dads do, isn't it?"

"No. Mom doesn't."

"Yeah, well, there you go."

Something's wrong with Jennifer. She's more blunt and distant than usual.

"Is there something you want to tell me, Jennifer?"

"Why was Mom crying when she picked me up?"

There it is.

"What did Mom say?" I ask.

"She said that you and she got into an argument in a

restaurant. She didn't want to talk any more about it right then."

I wait for her to continue.

"Is that true, Dad? Did you and Mom get into a fight?"

"It wasn't really a fight. But yeah, I kind of was a jerk again."

"Dad, what's wrong? Why do you get like that? Why do you get so angry?"

I motion to the screen. "Do you mind if I—" She nods. I grab the channel changer and turn the TV off. Then I sit down on the couch. She sits up. Both of us are now sitting on the couch facing forward, with several feet between us.

"What do you think, Jennifer? Why do you think I get so angry?"

"I don't know. But I really, really hate it when you get angry. I just want to run away to somewhere else."

I involuntarily slump and sigh deeply. "I'm sorry, Jennifer. I'm starting to hate it too. I think I'm getting better in some ways. But it takes so danged long. I really love your mom. None of this is her fault."

We're still facing forward.

"Dad, why don't you talk to me?"

"What do you mean? We talk."

"No, we don't. *You* talk. You tell me dad things you think you're supposed to say."

"Ouch," I say.

"We don't know each other, Dad. Mom and I talk all the time. She knows all my friends."

*I don't know what to say.*

"What do you want to talk about, Jennifer? I want to talk."

"Do you, Dad? Sometimes I don't think you do. You could come by my bedroom and knock, but you don't. Sometimes

I try to talk to you, but you usually seem somewhere else. I feel like I'm bothering you, or you're frustrated with me."

"Honey, I don't feel that way at all. Wow. I haven't read you well. I thought you didn't want me in your world. You really want me involved?"

"Yeah. Like right now there's a kid who I think likes me, and I don't have any idea what that's about. Sometimes Mom says, 'Go ask your dad. He's a boy.' But I don't ever feel like I can."

"Well, I'm an idiot."

"No, you're not. Sometimes I don't want to talk, you know."

"I've noticed." I'm looking fully at her now. She's still looking straight ahead.

"So, Jennifer, do you notice that when we talk, you don't look at me much?"

"I guess."

"So, why do you think that is?"

"I don't know," she says, still looking forward.

"Do you think it's maybe because you don't want to get hurt? And so you act like you don't care so much?"

"Maybe."

"Yeah. Maybe, huh. You know, kid, the funny thing is, I think you and I may be a lot alike. I'm finding out that most of what I do is to keep from getting hurt. You may have got some of that stuff from me. I'm sorry."

"It's all right."

All of a sudden, I am overwhelmed with an idea.

"You know what, kid? You could really help me. Maybe I could help you. Like when we get sad and afraid and we pull back. You know what I mean?"

"Yeah."

"Like maybe the other person could maybe say something. Or if we're around other people, maybe we could have a code or something. Like you could cough three times or something."

She laughs. For the first time tonight, Jennifer is looking at me, and she's smiling.

"I think I see what you meant a moment ago, Jennifer. We've never talked like this, have we?"

"No, we haven't, Dad."

"Would you do that, Jennifer? When you see me start to get weird? Do you know what I mean?"

"Yeah. You get this really goofy face. Your jaw gets all tight."

"So I've heard. Jen, for some reason it's hard for me to let your mom tell me. I blew it even today when she tried to stop me. It feels like I'm going to lose something. Maybe I don't trust that she has my back in the situation. And so then I power up. But you..."

"You really want me to?"

"I probably won't much like it at first. But I really do need you to do it. What do you say?"

"Yeah, I'll do it. But you gotta promise you'll listen to me when I do it... even if I'm wrong."

"I'll try, Jennifer."

"No. No trying. Promise me, Dad. Promise you'll listen and you'll stop."

*And so I give my daughter a promise I just broke today with my wife.*

"I promise, kid. But I may fight you at first."

"As long as you listen and stop."

I nod my head. "I can do that."

"Oh," she says. "And it can't be three coughs. I don't do that."

"What can you do, then?"

"I could whistle."

"All right. What would you whistle?"

She thinks for a second. "I could whistle the happy birthday song."

"That would be subtle. All right. That's it, then. Whenever I hear you whistling the happy birthday song, I need to just back off and shut it down until I get some objectivity. I like that. I'm in."

We shake hands with great exaggeration.

We're both looking at each other now, fully engaged.

"So, then, Jennifer..."

"Yeah?"

"What is my signal when I want to ask if you did your homework?"

"Nothing. Our signal will be nothing. Because I always do my homework. I've always done my homework, and you never, ever need to ask."

"Point taken. That's what I'll do then. I'll...do nothing. And you'll know when I do nothing that means I don't have to bother worrying about your homework."

"Exactly." We both laugh. She's now got her feet up on my knees.

We sit there for a while, saying nothing. We are just enjoying being dad and daughter. I finally break the silence.

"Well, I'm going to go write a note to your mom."

"That's a good idea, Dad."

"Hey, kid. Thank you for doing this."

"You're welcome, Dad."

We both stand up at the same time, and she gives me a hug, something I cannot remember receiving from her since she was a little girl. It takes me a long time to let go of her.

"Good night, kid."

"Good night, Dad." And she almost bounds up the stairs to her bedroom.

I stand there for some time in the dark. How long has she been wanting to tell me all that? Lindsey and I have an incredible daughter. Just another piece of my life I've been putting at risk. Geez.

I am caught off guard with tears. *I just trusted my daughter with me.* Then almost involuntarily, I whisper out loud, "Lindsey, I can do this. I can do this."

I find my way into the living room and turn on the muted green reading lamp at Lindsey's desk. I forage through the drawers until I find some nice stationery. I sit down and words begin pouring out.

Lindsey,

You usually get up before me, so I hope you read this before you see me.

Well, I did it again, huh? I hurt you again. I betrayed your trust...just as you were starting to risk again. I know saying "I'm sorry" won't work. I know I need to keep asking you to forgive me when I go out and do the same things over and over again. I really hate what I did to you today, Lindsey.

I think this is going to take a while. If you even let it go that far. I'm realizing there's stuff inside me—anger, screwed-up thinking, a bunch of junk from way back—that may take a while to get any better.

I didn't see it today... until it was too late. I really thought you were trying to sabotage the lunch. I know—crazy. Afterward, everyone around me let me know I was utterly and totally wrong. Andy said a while back, "When seven people tell you that you're drunk, you might want to find a place to lie down."

I knew, even while you were downstairs in Cynthia's car, that I had missed it completely.

I'm so sorry, Lindsey. You were just being you, which is wonderful. They all liked you so much. It was me they weren't so crazy about.

I sat at work tonight getting nothing done, really afraid that this time I may have finally scared you off. I'm asking God to let it not be too late. Here's all I can promise: I'm believing that God forgives me, even for today's craziness. This is all new to me. Even at this moment, it is so hard for me to dare allow myself to believe it.

Andy is about the wisest person I've ever met, and Cynthia has been his mentor. She really likes you. If you wanted to meet with her, I'd be good with that. And you can tell her anything you want.

Enough. Only this: I am so sorry for embarrassing you and making you feel like you aren't enough. You are everything to me. I am not well. You are the health and strength of this family. By the way, you wouldn't believe the conversation your daughter and I just had. She's an incredible girl. That's all about you, and God.

Lindsey, I'm asking again for your forgiveness. I am trusting Him to help me make things right. It's all I know how to do.

Love,

Steven

I fold the note and place it in an envelope, write her name across the front, and put it on top of the coffeemaker. Then I quietly crawl into bed next to my wife.

The next morning, I wait until she's had time to get to the coffee and read the note. Then I walk down the stairs and stand just outside the kitchen. She is still holding my note when she notices me. She makes no move, but a kind smile slowly works its way over her face.

"Thank you, Steven. I loved what you said." She says the next words as though she is risking a lot. "I'm here with you in this.... So, do you have that phone number for Cynthia? I think I would like to call her."

# "There Ain't No Together People, Just Those with Whiter Teeth."

*(Thursday Afternoon, June 4)*

Lindsey and Cynthia spent last Thursday afternoon together and have seen each other a couple of times this week. Each time, I get a little uneasy about what they must be saying. But a couple of phone calls to Andy and Carlos have helped get my thinking relatively straight again.

So here we are, back at Bo's. This time it's Lindsey's idea. She's catching the group up on what we've been talking through this past week.

"Steven and I have struggled in our marriage for a long time. Three weeks ago I was contemplating divorce. I've thought about it before, but this time I was actually playing it out in my head—where Jennifer and I would move, what kind of job I'd get. It was awful."

I'm listening, imagining how hard—even last week—it would have been to let her say those words to this group. To anyone. But now it doesn't seem that bad.

Cynthia laughs softly. "Steven, do you realize how amazing it is that you can let Lindsey say this to us?"

"Yeah, I guess. But it's pretty hard to sit here and be... pitied," I say.

"Oh, man!" Carlos responds. "No one at this table pities you. No one. We're all really sad she had to feel and think that junk. But look where you are. Surrounded by a table of friends getting to love and respect you like never before. You're letting us in, man. This is it. This is the good stuff. We're so proud of you."

Andy nods. "Every one of us at this table has stories of failure and immaturity like yours. Remember, all of us are learning to be convinced that if we have a safe place, where the worst about us can be known, the cycle of shame from old dead issues can be broken."

Cynthia adds, "I really think there is this great secret payoff for all those who give others permission to see behind the mask."

Once again she is awkwardly close to my face. "You find out the thing you feared the most never comes true. In fact, the opposite happens. You actually get to *be known*. You find out, in your vulnerability, that the *real* you is validated and loved."

Keith joins in. "When I was hidden, everybody was paying for it. Even if they didn't know it. Everybody was being robbed of the best of who I was. Even when I was on my game, I couldn't give you the real stuff God put inside me to give away. People wanted to love me, but they couldn't; people wanted me to love them, but I couldn't. Everybody lost."

Carlos jumps in. "Keith, you're on it, man. The goal is not just someone's exposure, but their freedom—so everyone gets the best of you. That's the deal."

Lindsey says, "Sometimes at church it feels like the ones who look all cleaned up are the admired ones. If you dare let someone know something wrong about you, it's like you're suddenly a second-class citizen, part of the leper group. You know what I mean? Who would dare let anyone in with those stakes?"

"You must have been attending my old church about five years ago." Carlos laughs. "Maybe you don't recognize me. I was thinner."

He stands up and pulls in his stomach.

"No, Carlos, it wasn't your church."

"A lot of churches," Carlos answers, "resemble that remark, Lindsey. But like my dad used to say, 'There ain't no together people. Just those with whiter teeth.' "

Cynthia stands up. "I think I was one of those people who could have made you feel that way. If we're not careful, we can do it here too. A well-dressed woman of maturity like myself can give the false impression of being above the common faults and failings of others. So, I guess it's my turn."

She takes a long drink from her water glass. "It's been nearly twenty-five years."

Cynthia then sets her glass back down on the table. "Keith and I had struggled for some time. We were married young and had almost no support base or instruction. Keith was a hotshot navy pilot. We spent two or three years in some of the hardest places in the world for a marriage to survive."

"Cyn and I had no clue," Keith says, reaching over and grabbing his wife's hand, her bracelets jingling. "We grew up in the same town in Kansas. I had known Cynthia since I was six. At some point, on one of our times home from college, we just realized we were in love."

"He told me he knew since fifth grade that we would get married."

"After college Cynthia and I got married and were immediately stationed in Norfolk, Virginia. Then Annapolis, San Diego, back to Norfolk, and the Gulf Coast—all within two years. We just thought everything would work out, somehow."

"It didn't," Cynthia adds flatly. "I was unhappy and depressed. Oh, and I was sure to let him hear about it all the time. I didn't know how to make friends with military wives. Most of them were so...well, military. And they thought I was some kind of hippie art kook. And Keith was away so much of the time."

Keith takes over. "I was spending more and more time in town with officers just as young, stupid, restless, and frustrated as I was. I started telling Cynthia I was held up after work for briefings with the commanding officer or some such bunk."

Cynthia looks down at Keith. "After a while I knew he was lying, but I couldn't bring myself to face it. I wonder now how may of the lies I helped him create. The poor guy couldn't win. When he didn't come home, I was miserable and let him know it. When he *did* come home, I was miserable and let him know it. Oh, I was a regular witch."

"Most of you know the rest of the story," Keith continues. "Trouble knows how to find someone hanging out in the same room. It was one night, one stupid act. It was never about being in love with another woman. I was just so immature and disappointed with my life. I gave myself permission to do something very wrong, and somehow, at least in the moment, almost felt vindicated in doing it. And, of course, I hid it from her."

*It's hard to believe I'm sitting here on this deck, listening to these two sharing something as intimate as this.*

"We drifted further and further apart," Cynthia explains. "Our double bed seemed like three king-size beds." She stops for a beat before she continues.

"Then one evening, at a going-away party just before we were being transferred yet again, I overheard an offhand remark from a pilot friend of Keith's who'd had way too much to drink. I confronted Keith when we got home. He confessed. I came completely undone. Whatever illusions

I'd had of a happy marriage dissolved in that instant. I felt anger, embarrassment, disgust, and fear, all in the same moment. I was suddenly a victim. And Keith represented all that destroyed my childhood dreams.

"Oh, and I was hurt that God knew and didn't let me know sooner. So I was a victim with no one to run to."

Keith's eyes have clouded with emotion.

"It tore me up to see what I had done to her," he says. "I grew up in a Christian home, but I think that was the first time I ever took God seriously. I cried out to Him, day after day. I got help from a base chaplain and his wife. I repented to God and to Cyn. It was an incredibly wrenching experience. But I gradually grew to believe that God had forgiven me. Cynthia and I tried to get back to some form of normalcy in our marriage, but even after a long time something still wasn't right."

"What was it?" Lindsey asks.

"I became convinced I was a better person than Keith. I reasoned that I *never* would have or could have done something like what he did. I was better than that. I was a better person."

She is walking now behind Keith's chair.

"And I held it over him. God was freeing him from bondage, and at home I was retying all the knots. I thought I had to be in control to get my life back. And so I thought my job was to keep him in a perpetual state of penance.

"It worked. He became convinced that in order to regain trust, he had to take the abuse of my arrogant superiority. I leveraged that control over him in a hundred ways. I used it to manipulate his behavior and ensure that he never forgot what he owed me for staying."

She sits back down, her ringing bracelets the only sound on the deck.

"And slowly life leaked out of my husband. He became a

well-behaved, compliant little boy, always trying to stay out of the doghouse. I couldn't see that I was robbing myself of my husband a second time."

Cynthia looks directly at Lindsey. "My dear new friend, I fear there are thousands of husbands and wives living in similar prisons. One fails, and the other finds control by never letting the other feel free and restored. It destroys two lives. One is kept pitifully pinned down while the other is trapped in arrogant blindness, allowed to ignore their own debilitating issues."

Lindsey has been very quietly taking this all in. "So, what changed?"

Cynthia looks steadily at Keith as she responds. "One evening I was looking at my husband. He was sitting across from me in our living room, watching television. I happened to be browsing through a photo album, looking at pictures of the two of us. One picture was from soon after we were married. He was full of life, mischief, and playful affection. And oh, dear, he was so handsome! He was messing with my hair, looking at me with such confident delight. It looked like he was about to say something funny or take me in his arms and dip me, or tell me about some exotic place he was going to take us on leave....

"Then I put down the album and stared at the stranger on my couch. He looked old, empty, and tired.

"Over time I had succeeded in convincing him that he wasn't the man in that picture. I'd taught him he was a hollow failure whose highest aim should be to try, over a lifetime, to earn his way back into my favor. For years I'd seen him as weak and in need of my control. In that moment I gained a glimpse of how much I had hurt him, forcing him to become that hollow man. But I wouldn't allow myself to stay there. For I had lost the ability to allow myself to hurt for him. To do that, I'd have to face my own sins. Oh, and, dear one, I was not ready for that. But from that moment on, it began to haunt me.

"Eventually God sent me an older woman who had the courage to ask, 'So, Cynthia, how does Keith's failure reflect on you?' In a moment I realized that my own deep shame had caused me to be publicly embarrassed by my husband. The pain from his actions had left a long time ago. I wasn't a victim of his sexual failure; I was the victim *of my own shame*. My friend began to help me uncover the lies that would cause such a distorted nine-year-long response."

A waiter has been refreshing iced tea glasses around the table. He is taking his time, drawn into the story.

"Thank you, Cynthia," Lindsey says, reaching out for my hand. "I do not want to go down that road."

Cynthia puts her hand on both of ours. "That's why we're here."

I feel a wave of gratitude for this place, for these people. "I've got to believe," I say, "there are a whole lot of people who need friends like this."

"No doubt," Andy answers. "The writers of the New Testament talked a lot about it. They actually imagined churches that would be this way."

I answer quickly. "Not likely. *I've* never seen churches like that."

"*I* have," Hank says, coaxing ketchup out of a bottle with a french fry.

"You're kidding yourself, Hank," I say. "Church doesn't work that way. They're institutions. And what self-respecting pastor would hang out with a crowd like this? Too much risk to his reputation."

Andy tilts his head and says, "Well, now, that's odd, because I'd swear I see *Carlos* here almost every week."

Carlos says nothing; he just grins back at me.

"I'm sorry, Carlos. That was a stupid statement. Sometimes I forget you're a pastor."

"So do I," he responds. "It's something I'm working on, though."

"But you're not like this at church, are you?"

"What do you mean?" he asks, genuinely puzzled.

"Well, I just mean, how do you reconcile, I mean, how much does your church know about some of what you shared with me that day a while back. You know, I mean... they don't know about the way you are around here—do they?"

Carlos is suddenly very serious. "Steven, do you think we're doing something wrong here?"

"What?" I ask.

"Is Jesus happy with what goes on here in this little gig? Is this right and good, what we're doing?"

"I think as right as anything I've ever done."

"Then you tell me, Steven, why wouldn't this be fit for a church?"

I go silent, not wanting to make a bigger fool of myself.

"Steven, this is not a game, man," Carlos says, leaning in to me. "We're not playing hooky, you know? Carlos has to be the same cat in a hotel on the road as he is praying in front of people on Sunday. Otherwise we're just playing *dress-up,* man. This is me, Steven. I don't get no more religious than this. Lotsa people probably wish I would. I just don't think God is one of them. You know?

"Listen, we don't need places like this to become more like church. We need churches to become more like this place. You know?"

"I think I do, Carlos. I'm sure sorry for what I said earlier. You're as self-respecting a pastor as I've ever known."

"Thanks, man. That means a lot to me." Carlos smiles warmly.

"So, Carlos, does everyone on the deck crowd go to your church?" I ask.

"Oh, no, man, are you kidding? Would you want to go to church with Hank?"

Everyone laughs, and Hank just nods sheepishly.

We are interrupted by Bo shouting something to an employee, then laughing his big, barrel-chested laugh. It seems to signal the end of our time together. Carlos says his good-byes. Hank takes our pile of cash and debit cards up to the front register. Cynthia stands up, gives Andy and me big hugs, and then walks over to my wife and sits next to her.

"How are you feeling about all this, Lindsey?"

"Hopeful, I think."

"Lindsey, this whole regaining of trust doesn't come overnight. There will be some hard times. Steven will fail again. He will explode in anger again. And you'll feel the same fear all over again. But something else is happening too. Your husband, I think, is beginning to humble his heart. So God is now free every moment to let his new story begin to dominate his experience. That will change everything."

Standing behind my wife as Cynthia says this, I put my hands on Lindsey's shoulders and say, "I want to say this in front of you guys. Lindsey, you have my permission to let Cyn or Hank or Andy or anybody know when you think I'm starting to get out of control. No more secrets. No more hiding."

Cynthia adds, "You'll need to find others, who can stand with you as you begin to risk learning how to open your heart again. I'd be honored to be one you can grow to count on. This doesn't have to take nine years. We just didn't have anyone. You guys have all this in front of you. You just have to let others care for you."

Lindsey grasps Cynthia's hand. "Thank you, Cynthia. You've been great. This is all so new. I don't know what's coming for our family. I'm hopeful, but it's scary too."

For a moment all the strangeness returns. This is all because of me. Everyone's stepping to the plate to meet with my wife because of what *I've* done. I feel like a recovering monster, still capable of wiping out a community with a single swipe. It's hard to believe this new identity when I am daily faced with the living consequences of the old one.

But I look over at Andy. He's smiling at me. I've learned the meaning behind that smile.

*Don't be afraid. I know who you are. You know too much to listen to the lies now. Nothing to come can change that. I've got your back.*

I smile back.

*Thank you. Thank you for being my friend.*

# "I Was Playing You Like a Gibson Hummingbird."

*(Friday, December 4)*

The last few years I'd grown to really dislike Christmas. A whole month to magnify how unhappy Lindsey and I were. A month to regret. A month to bluff. This season is different. The pressure and tension are mostly gone.

Last Saturday, I actually put up Christmas lights out front—by myself. First time ever. As a kid, Dad always did them, by himself. I could stand by and watch if I wanted, but I always felt like I was in the way. I could get him a hammer or steady the ladder, but I was never allowed to put up the lights with him. By the time I got in junior high, I just avoided the whole painful event. I think he was just insecure about the whole deal. Mr. Magnusson, across the street, always had this incredible animated display. He had deer with moving heads before you could buy them in the stores.

In recent years I've always had neighborhood kids string up the lights for money. Not this year. I put 'em up. They've looked better. It definitely looks like a rookie put them up. But I like them kind of loosely hanging there, a little uneven, but happy. Kind of like our lives now. Not so tied down—like our old displays: they were nice and neat-appearing for the neighbors, but stiff, tight, and cold if you got up close. And I didn't use those trendy white twinkle lights. I went out and found some of those big, beautiful, bright, old-school bulbs. Andy decks out some of the boats in the marina with them. He says they're C9s. He tells me they're the Christmas bulbs the apostles used back in the day.

This afternoon Andy and I are once again in the Electra. We catch the 405 and take the off-ramp up into the familiar hills overlooking Marina del Rey and Venice. Once again he parks the car, facing south, on the same bluff as the first time we came up here. He turns off the lights and then the engine. He takes a long draw from his half-finished cigar, blowing an impressive smoke ring into the cool evening air. I am wearing his Dodgers warm-up jacket. His accommodation to the weather is a long-sleeved T-shirt under his ever-present Hawaiian shirt.

"So...?" he tosses out into the night air, as if I'm supposed to fill in the rest.

I take the bait.

"Andy, do you know the first evening we came up here, I still wasn't sure who you were, or what you were up to? I thought to myself, *This is how it happens. You hear about it all the time. 'Promising executive chopped to pieces by serial ax murderer.'* "

After another smoke ring he replies, "Do you know that first evening, I wasn't completely certain I wasn't wasting my time? You, my friend, were a real piece of work."

"Me? I wasn't the one acting all Nostradamus-like. You could have told me about the name tag right away, but no-o-o! You wait until I threaten to call the manager!"

"Oh, that was poetry!" Andy slaps his knee. "I was playing you like a Gibson Hummingbird, I was."

Then we are quiet, content to look out over Los Angeles at night. Looking down into the basin toward the ocean, I try to guess which lights might belong to Bo's Café. The last six months, since we all met that afternoon on the deck, have radically changed my whole world. It's been the best six months of my life.

Andy and I continue to meet. I'm now a regular at Bo's. I'm even bringing a friend from work on occasion. Lindsey and I are now part of Carlos's church in Hermosa Beach. And I am slowly learning to believe this new DNA God built into me. Lindsey is slowly learning to trust again. I am still more than capable of returning to the old lies. And when I do, I can still hurt my wife and anyone around me. But there hasn't been a single day when I've walked out to the parking lot feeling like I can't go home.

I rest my hands behind my head. I am searching for words. I want to say something that will convey just how much he has meant to me. But everything sounds trite and insufficient.

"So what have you learned since we first came up here?" he asks.

I pull my gaze away from the lights and look over at him.

"You're kidding, right?"

"Fair enough. Then give me something you're learning right now."

"Well, first, I owe you about two hundred apologies for all the arrogant things I said and thought about you. I had you pegged for the longest time as an eccentric, kindly loser. Fascinating, insightful, but still a bit of a loser. Andy, I gave myself permission to discount about half of what you were telling me just because of where you worked, how you dressed, where you lived. How could anything you might say possibly apply to me?"

Andy nods and grins. "I think I knew that from the first evening."

"Hey, Andy, you got a few more minutes? There's someone I've been trying to help at work."

"Sure, I'm just a middle-class guy working at a marina. What else have I got to do? Go home and watch reruns of *Cops*?"

"You're not ever going to let me forget that, are you?"

"Nope."

"Her name's Meagan. She's kind of a whiz kid. Until recently she was a designer down on the first floor. But this kid's got incredible talent. She was the lead on our last two big video-game best sellers. Last year she took her team through a design concept for a hockey game that has already gotten out into the market. It's actually started to change the way animators describe movement. She can't be twenty-five."

Andy sits up. "It's about time you people got someone improving that. The animation in most games looks like 'Great Moments with Mr. Lincoln' at Disneyland back a few years. Lincoln would bend his arms in ways that weren't humanly possible. He was like Gumby in a stovepipe hat. I'm sure he frightened the children. He always freaked me out."

"Uh . . . stay with me here, Andy. Anyway, this kid's a mess. She's more arrogant than me. If she wasn't so talented, she'd already be gone. Meagan's already had run-ins with several executive team members. Last month she publicly called out the head of operations to fix a 'ridiculously flawed system' or she'd go elsewhere. Visratech doesn't want to lose her, but she's getting increasingly hard to keep."

"So?"

"So, the kid comes to me two weeks ago. Walks into my office and says, 'Mr. Kerner, I think I need your help.'

"Inside I'm thinking, *My help? I'm the one who's about to have to can you.*

"The conversation goes something like this:

" 'I don't know if word's getting back to you,' she says, 'but I'm not doing well with the big dogs.'

" 'I've maybe heard a few things... in passing.'

" 'Well, anyway, Mr. Kerner, I kind of watch you.'

" 'You do?'

" 'Yep. I do. You didn't used to come down to the first floor much. And when you did, you always had this condescending, forced smile. Like you were thinking, *Well, aren't these little people working hard. Bless their hearts, each and every one of them.*'

" 'Speak your mind. Don't hold back, Meagan.'

" 'What I'm trying to say is that something's changed. You hang out. You don't have that stupid smile as often. You don't come off like you're better than us. You ask us for help. And you're starting to listen to us.'

" 'Thanks, Meagan. I think.'

" 'So I'm thinking, *If I'm gonna have a chance to make it here, maybe this guy can help me.*'

" 'You want *my* help?'

" 'I know you're really busy. But I've got a chance to do something I've wanted to do all my life. And now that I'm here, I'm screwing it all up. I always have, Mr. Kerner. Will you help me? I can't fail at this.' "

Andy is listening intently while savoring the last inches of his cigar.

"She goes on to tell me about her relationship with her dad. They don't talk; haven't for six years. She says he doesn't even know about her success with the new video games. It's killing her. Andy, I really like this kid. I see a lot of me in her. But I have no idea what to tell her. I just want to say the right things to fix her. But I don't know how to fix her. The last thing this kid needs is another authority letting her down. Do you have any experience in this?"

"Other than with the marketing VP of the company she works for? Duh, nope."

"You know what I mean. Would you help me?"

"Steven, in my office at the marina I have this statement tacked up on the wall: *'Integrity is proven when you admit what you cannot do and honor what you say you can.'*

"What do you think that means?"

"I repeat to myself, '...*when you admit what you cannot do*...'

"I think you're saying that bluffing and trying to make Meagan think I have all the answers will cause her to not trust the answers I *do* have."

"Good answer. Very good answer." He pauses for a moment.

"Steven, do you remember the first time I brought you to Bo's? You asked me what my real issues were. I never answered you that day."

"I noticed."

"Steven, my dad has been my issue from the time I was seventeen. No, probably from the time I was five. Classic father from that generation. It's like they all took the same course, used the same formula: Withhold affirmation, expect what no one can do, and then give a nonverbal response that communicates disappointment. Nothing I did was good enough, fast enough, or successful enough.

"When I was a kid, he used to let me wash the car with him. One day, when I was about seven, he asked if I wanted to dry it off. It was a big deal. He never let me dry it. I worked so hard on that car. When I got done, while I was still standing there, *he completely redid it.*"

Andy is staring out into space, looking as if he's been transported back to that moment.

"It's crazy that I still remember it so clearly. The garden hose was red. I was wearing a green shirt with stripes. Steven, what I did, who I was, was never enough.

"From early on, there was this message continually running around in my head: *if I could just do this or accomplish this, Dad would finally be proud of me.* Eventually I did things not out of love for him, but to prove that I was worthy of his praise. It's wired into us. A dad becomes that barometer of worth for a kid—boy or girl. If we don't get affirmation or acceptance, we can walk through life grasping for it and demanding it out of almost everyone. People in authority don't have a chance with us. We demand so much out of them, trying to rewrite what we didn't get. They're always set up to fail us.

"So, I learned to never fail but to win...and then some. It caused me to blur the lines of integrity just to make sure I didn't lose my place. It drove me to be right at all costs. To see others as in my way or as enemies to be defeated. It eventually, predictably, drove me to character failure.

"For decades I was certain he was my life issue. If I could just get him to change, to own, to understand. If I could learn to not care about his criticisms; if I could finally achieve something that would once and for all settle the issue of my worth....

"But ultimately, he wasn't my issue. *I* was my issue. I was bullying my way through life, trying to be enough to overcome another's assessment of me. That's what Cynthia and Keith could see.

"Meagan isn't that different from anyone else. She's just another on an endless conveyor belt of those who've been trapped into believing a lie about themselves."

As he tells his own story, I see myself, I see Meagan, I see hundreds of others. Lies picked up when we're young can stay with us a lifetime.

I look over at Andy and shake my head.

He asks, "What?"

I answer, "Thanks. That's all."

"For what?"

"For being a good man. You really could have screwed me up. But you didn't. You're helping break some pretty deep patterns, just by being who you said you were."

"Yeah, well, you're welcome, kid. It's been a good ride."

Andy starts up the Electra. And we're off, rumbling slowly back down the hill. Once again I am aware of the feel of the leather seat, the wind lifting my shirt. He pops a CD out of the player I recently had installed for him.

"I love these things!" he shouts to me over the wind and engine. "They're so shiny! What'll it be? B. B. King?"

I pull down the sun visor and grab U2's *The Joshua Tree* out of the disc holder.

"This time I pick," I tell him, handing him the CD and replacing the other.

He grins and takes a big puff off his cigar as the music starts up.

I love this. I hope these rides in this ridiculous giant boat never end.

# And Back Again

*(Saturday Morning, December 19)*

Lindsey and I are awakened by a loud knock at the door. The clock says 6:22. I stumble downstairs and open the front door. Hidden behind several grocery bags is—Andy.

"You gonna let me in, or should I make breakfast out here on the lawn?"

I am yet unable to form words, so I point him toward the kitchen.

Unpacking what looks like a cappuccino maker, he says, "I wasn't sure you folks made coffee at home, so I took the liberty. I used to think this whole overpriced steamed-coffee deal was a marketer's gimmick. But if you haven't savored a well-made breve latte with a hint of cinnamon, well, children, put down the manna. We are about to cross over the Jordan!"

Several minutes later Lindsey shuffles into the kitchen. By now Andy is pouring juice.

"Good morning, Lindsey," Andy says. "Is Jenny up yet?"

"Hello, Andy." She walks over and gives him a hug. "Jennifer's still asleep. Might I ask what we're doing?"

"Well, I'm getting out of town for the holidays. It gets a little dicey this time of year for a widower. Lonely isn't so lonely if you're in a place where you're not supposed to have family. So, I mix it up each year. Palm Springs this time. But I didn't want to leave without saying Merry Christmas to one of my favorite families.

"My clan is originally from Norway," he says as he opens the oven door. "This recipe for cherry streusel was handed down to me from many generations back. I make it every Christmas. So this year I make it for you."

Lindsey immediately understands the importance of the moment.

"Oh, Andy. Thank you." She hugs him again.

Within minutes the two of them are bustling around like an old married couple, setting the table, folding fancy napkins, and cooking up eggs and sausage. Eventually I'm invited to the table. They are already seated. Andy takes off his ball cap, clears his throat, and asks, "May I?"

Lindsey answers, "We'd be honored, Andy."

"Precious God," he prays, "thanks for this. You are the giver of everything good. And You are giving the three of us really good lives. You have given us Jesus. And so much has beautifully changed. I do not know where I would be without His love."

He pauses a bit as though he's imagining his life without God in it.

"And thanks for letting me meet Steven that night at Fenton's. Thank You for letting me be part of this beautiful family.

"Anyway, we love You and thank You for letting Him come breathe our air, letting Him bring the broken home. Amen."

Over the next hour, amid streusel and lattes, we replay how we got to this day. Lindsey recalls the day she was introduced to Andy, laughing about her trendy fashion sunglasses that passed as vintage. We laugh about Bo's. It's the kind of unguarded playfulness that was absent from our home for so long.

Eventually Andy asks, "So, Lindsey, how are you doing? I

talk to Steven, but I want to know how you think things are going. You and Steven."

Lindsey turns from the kitchen counter, where she is cutting slices of streusel, and moves up behind me. She places her hands on my shoulders, facing Andy across the table.

"That's not an easy question to answer. In some ways it can be almost harder than it was before. I'm realizing I can set myself up to believe I'm not ever going to get hurt again, that Steven is done with his anger. But he can still ramp up. Not nearly as often or as bad. But when he does, because I'm opening up again, the hurt can feel almost worse than before. Does that make sense?"

"Perfect sense." Andy nods.

"But our relationship is so much better, in ways I never even counted on. It's more real and alive and true."

I reach up for her hand and squeeze it.

"You know my favorite moments? It's when Steven catches himself getting wound up and he calls time-out. He'll actually stop the conversation and say something like, 'This is about me right now, huh?' And I'll smile and say, 'Well, yeah, maybe kind of.' And he'll say, 'I really think I had a point going there, and I'm pretty sure I thought I was right, but I'm going to have to let it go for now. Thanks.' "

"Some of the time," I add, "I'm stopping because of Jennifer. She and I have a signal, Andy. It's really pretty amazing. She doesn't use it unless I'm starting to look like the Hulk."

"Very cool, very cool," Andy says as he leans back in his chair, deeply enjoying our reflections.

"Anyway," Lindsey continues, "he just asks to hold me. In those moments, everything gets stronger. I gain hope and trust. And he starts to believe he can live this way. And I'm learning to not take advantage of his vulnerability. I sort of did early on. Andy, that's when it becomes about me, huh?"

"Yeah, I think so."

Lindsey continues, "I can't demand Steven to never fail again. I can't control his every action, or I'll become someone I don't like. And Steven will wither into a well-behaved, empty shell. And he has so much more to offer than being the 'passive, controlled guy.' "

"Lindsey's also made some good friends at church," I add. "And we've gotten close to several couples. We're starting to let them know about our struggles. I think that's been a safety net for Lindsey."

"This is the church at its best. See, if you don't have the safety of those friends to air it out with, it's really hard for Steven to get healthy. Everything gets strange in the vacuum of privacy."

Lindsey now wraps her arms more tightly around me and presses her head next to mine.

"Andy, I want you to know what else I see in my husband. I see courage. I'm realizing these issues didn't all start with him. This is a pattern that goes way back in the Kerner family. In his love for Jenny and me, he's facing some really hard stuff."

She sits down in the chair next to me and touches my face. "Steven, do you know that because you are risking to trust God and others with you, that you are giving your daughter a healthier life? Did you know that? You can't have any idea how much that means to me. Jenny will get to grow up knowing what a good man looks like. How a healthy man faces his issues. She is watching your humility. She is watching you let me love you. You know what?" She shakes her head in amazement. "Her children will be healthier than us. And they will never know why. But I will, Steven. I will."

A mischievous smile forms on Lindsey's face.

"You know what I'd like?" she says, clapping her hands together like a young girl.

"I'd like you to ask me out on a date for tonight. You will take me to an extravagant restaurant, and we will eat a ridiculously expensive meal. I will order their nicest glass of red wine. And we will embarrass other nearby couples with our obvious affection. Then you will drive us home. I'll light some candles, while you put on some romantic music. I will tell you how proud I am of you. Then you will tell me how beautiful I look."

She giggles. "You will do that part throughout the evening."

Andy winks at me.

"Then you will thank me for hanging in there with you all these years. And then, once again, you will bring up the part about how beautiful I look."

Lindsey *is* beautiful. She was always attractive, but over these last six months she has become incredibly beautiful to me.

I stand and pull her up to me, taking her into my arms. "You know what I think I'd like us to do? We need to go out tonight, to a really expensive restaurant. What do you think?"

Our faces inches from each other, she says, "That's a great idea. I'd love to."

Andy finally speaks. "Have you ever felt like you needed to be hosed off just listening to a couple plan a date?" He loosens an imaginary tie and fans himself.

"You know what? I've got an idea. If you'd like, we can trade cars for a few days. It seems fitting. Steven, when we started this journey, I told you that the Electra could take you to the places you needed to go. Right now it sounds like that might be a romantic seaside hideaway somewhere up Highway 1."

"Yes!" Lindsey shouts, throwing her arms around Andy.

"Plus," he adds, "I'll be driving the Mercedes. Folks in Palm Springs will stare at me tooling down the boulevard, wondering which L.A. celebrity I am."

Twenty minutes later I'm standing in the driveway holding the keys to a 1970 Buick Electra, while a homeless-looking man in flip-flops and a Hawaiian shirt slides behind the wheel of my Mercedes.

He pulls away in my car, yelling loudly enough to wake all the neighbors, "Enjoy the Electra. I'll be back in town early the week after Christmas. Just drop her by my house on your way to work one day. Merry Christmas! Ho, ho, ho!"

By the time I turn back around from watching Lindsey's reaction, he's gone.

# "I Have Waited for This Moment All Week."

*(Tuesday Morning, December 29)*

I'm driving over to Andy's house, sad to be giving up his car. It's one thing to ride in a 1970 Buick Electra convertible; it is something else all together to commandeer one. Talk about old school. Behind the giant steering wheel, with its loose play and ridiculous turn radius, you can't decide if you should round up some buddies and go rob a bank or pick up the homecoming queen and drive her around a track.

Today, dressed in a tie, I feel like a character from an old Sinatra movie, on the Vegas Strip, making his way to the Dunes to rough up someone with his brass knuckles.

But, alas, today Andy and I are exchanging cars.

At least that's what he thinks.

I have waited for this moment all week. Maybe I have waited for this moment my whole life. Some call what is about to happen *convergence.* Andy calls it the *true legacy of exchange.* This is the stuff you expect to see only in movies. And now it is happening in my world. How crazy. Before the world began, God showed the angels this whole scene on tape delay, and now it takes place on earth. This is what Andy has waited for all along. He's been modeling the necessary destination of the very relationship he initiated. He knew that for it to be authentic, someday, in some areas, the student would have to become the teacher. The one being protected would become the protector. This is the life Andy led me into. This is what I have matured into. He's been working toward this since the day we met! He just didn't know it would happen like this.

I cannot wait to see the expression on his face.

I have my Oakleys on, the ones with glare-resistant lenses and unbreakable frames. I've called ahead, asking him to be outside when I pull up. I'm very, very good, if I do say so myself.

I turn onto his street and spot him off in the distance, standing out front, next to my Mercedes.

*Here we go.*

I pull up next to the Mercedes, out in the middle of the street. I put the car in park, the engine still running.

He looks at me, confused. "What's going on?"

We both stare at each other. I say nothing. I just smile and put my right arm on top of the seat. I'm suddenly flooded with a blur of experiences he and I have shared on this amazing ride.

*Threatening him at Fenton's. Driving us up on the hill, blowing smoke rings into the night air. Hearing his voice as the sound track for the scenes below I was starting to see for the first time. Talking me out of my own house, over the phone. Walking me through my first visit to Bo's. Listening to him describe his business failure. Watching me, in my office, trapping myself. Holding cups of coffee at the marina. Letting go of the wheel, out on the ocean. Confronting my lies after I hurt Lindsey at lunch. Sitting next to him as he bares his soul about his dad. Waking up to him on our doorstep behind shopping bags holding ingredients for his Norwegian streusel.*

"Steven?"

I am so excited I can barely say it with a straight face. "Good morning, Andy. Get in."

He's taken aback. "What do you mean? Where are we going?"

"We're going to go see your dad."

Andy is expressionless.

"You're going to need these." I toss him a pair of my Oakleys.

Andy tries to say something to buy time. "Uh, what do you . . . you mean right *now*? Because I was going to . . ."

"Look, I'm pretty sure this car will take us to the places you need to go. But I can't make you get in."

"But I thought we were gonna exchange cars today."

That's when I give him the answer I've rehearsed all week long. "I can't, Andy. At least not on your terms. So are you getting in, or am I gonna buy you a pound of coffee and send you on your way?"

*Ka ching.*

He looks at me a long time. Then he looks down, his hands in his pockets, gently kicking at the ground. The exchange is taking place, only now in reverse. Like a boomerang, what Andy threw out as a gift has finally found its way back to him.

Then he looks up at me, almost smiling.

"You're good. You're very good. All right, Steven, let's go see my dad."

Go figure. Andy is letting me protect *him*.

Andy reaches in to open the door with the inside handle. He puts on my Oakleys and sits down in the passenger seat. He runs his hands along the seat, and then sits back as far as he can, settling in for a ride down the coast.

He pulls out a cigar and begins to unwrap it. "Do you mind if I smoke?" he asks.

"Yes, I do." I don't, really. I've just wanted the chance to say that for so long.

I caught him off guard, just as I'd hoped. He answers quickly. "Oh, yes, well, sure. Sorry." He puts the cigar back into his shirt and continues, "You're right. I've been trying to quit. I really am going to quit."

And with that the giant Electra convertible rumbles its way out of his neighborhood.

Two prodigals, with vastly different journeys, are together again, finding their way back home.

# Acknowledgments

We are grateful to those who continue to teach us God's grace in spite of what is true about us, and for those who introduced us to his dreams for our lives and now stand with us as we are privileged to share truths with others.

Thanks to our loyal board of directors, our dedicated staff, our generous financial partners, our advisory council, and the friends of TrueFaced for your timeless encouragement and sacrificial investments. We especially thank Amber Ong Kakimoto, Rod Gipson, Doris Wescott, Jason Lehman, David Pinkerton, Shannon McCarthy, and Steve and Carol Barger, in whose mountain home many of these pages were penned.

Most significantly, we thank Toben Heim, our media director at TrueFaced Resources & Leadership Catalyst. Toben shepherded this project through its last year with editorial, marketing, and publishing savvy that we three coauthors didn't possess. Like us, this TrueFaced message of *Bo's Café* has rescued Toben's life. Toben, you are a rare blend!

Without the invitation of William Young we would never have met our collaborators and publishers at Windblown. Wayne Jacobsen, Brad Cummings, and Mick Silva—you have been an unexpected gift of immense significance. Thank you for your storytelling ways, your editorial nuance, and your generosity.

We uniquely appreciate our friend Bob Ryan, a gifted playwright and musician, who again owes his life to the truths embodied in *Bo's Café*. Bob, your exquisite literary "catches" add intrigue and energy to this story.

Thanks to the men and women of Sharky Productions theater troupe, Open Door Fellowship, the Neighborhood Church, Spring Mountain Bible Church, and EBMMAS (the Ernest Borgnine Memorial Music Appreciation Society), with whom we are privileged to enjoy community and live in these truths.

We are grateful to the more than fifty volunteer readers, researchers, media experts, and storytellers who love this message and use their talents to propel this incredible message of God's grace: people like Nathan Mates, Bob Snow, Kathy Deering, Mike Hamel, and Jason Pearson, who contributed their insights, critique, or substantial refinement to *Bo's Café*.

Thanks to the men and women who followed God's nudge in their lives, embraced these truths, and now represent that diverse group around the world on which the story of *Bo's Café* is based.

Finally, we thank our wives and families, who are the most loving and faithful mirrors of these truths in our lives, both when we are living in them and when we stray from them.

# Personal Message from the Authors

## Sharing This Book with Others

If you have been encouraged by the message of grace and life change contained in these pages and would like to share it with others, here are some ideas and easy ways to help.

- We will be blogging on www.boscafe.com at least once a week. Come by and check it out. We'll have plenty of stories to tell about how this message is spreading. Leave us a comment and tell us your grace-story!
- Be our friend on Facebook. Just search for **Bo's Café Book** and you'll find us. We promise to confirm you as a friend! This is a great way to stay in touch with what's going on with the book and the authors.
- We know many of you have blogs, Facebook pages, and Twitter accounts. We'd love to have you post a review of the book along with a link to www.boscafe.com. You can also leave your thoughts at Amazon.com. Your recommendation is all many will need to pick up the book and start their journey.
- Create a simple button or use a JPEG of the cover on your Web site or blog with a link to www.boscafe.com. This is the easiest way for your friends, family, and readers to start their own journey into grace.
- Buy a few copies to give away. We have a friend who takes a copy of the book on the plane with him just so he can

leave it in a seat-back pocket for whoever sits there next. Another friend gives a copy away to her server in restaurants. Of course you can give them to people you know well too!

- If you have a great opportunity for one of our authors to appear on your local radio station, morning TV show, or in a local print publication, send us an e-mail at boscafe@boscafe.com and let us know about it. We'll take it from there, providing a review copy and other information to help them make their decision to help us spread the word.
- We can't travel and speak in all the places we wish we could, but if you have an opportunity for one of our authors to speak at your church, your organization, or conference, send us an e-mail at boscafe@boscafe.com and we'll see what we can arrange.

Our prayer is that more and more people will come to discover the life and freedom in Christ that living in his grace affords us. We have given our lives to helping people move into relationships and environments of grace where they can be authentic and who they were created to be. Thanks for your part in passing along the opportunity to live a grace-filled life!

# About the Authors

## John Lynch

As a great communicator and a talented writer, John Lynch is a vital member of the Leadership Catalyst/TrueFaced community. John has coauthored a number of books and resources with Bill and Bruce, including the bestseller *True-Faced* and the popular *TrueFaced* audio-video message.

## Bill Thrall

As vice chair and coauthor for Leadership Catalyst/True-Faced, Bill has a desire to see relational health in those he works with. His eloquence and integrity have given him opportunities to teach these principles internationally. His wisdom has been penned throughout the entire series of The Ascent of a Leader, Beyond Your Best, and TrueFaced Experience books.

## Bruce McNicol

As cofounder and president of Leadership Catalyst/True-Faced, Bruce has a passion to see tens of thousands of safe places like Bo's Café established around the world, whether they are families, businesses, schools, hospitals, churches, organizations, sports teams, the military, or governments.

Bruce's degrees in finance law, theology, leadership, and organizational development helped hone his gift to speak to the lives of others, which continues to draw international audiences.

*Coming soon from Windblown Media*

*Newbury Park, California*

***The Misunderstood God: The Lies Religion Tells Us About God*** by Darin Hufford

Is there more to God than meets the religious eye? From the publishers of *The Shack* comes a provocative book that further unveils the unfathomable love and grace of God. Author Darin Hufford takes God's claim to be love itself and holds it up against God's own definition of love in one of the most beloved passages of the Bible—1 Corinthians 13. Scripture calls him the God of love, but religion often portrays him with the vindictive personality of the devil. Which one is he and how can we be sure? If you've ever struggled to understand the nature of God, this book will help you come to see that God is truly the definition of love.

***Compelling stories that unveil God's heart to the spiritually curious***

***www.windblownmedia.com***

(805) 498-2484